A MAKEOVER MADE IN HEAVEN

SHARON SROCK

A BLONDE AND A PRAYER BOOKS

Cover Design by Mallory Rock of www.RockSolidBookDesign.com

❀ Created with Vellum

Blake and Trinity: May God bless your marriage and the little one you carry.

Psalms 13:5-6
But I have trusted in Your lovingkindness; My heart shall rejoice in Your Salvation. I will sing to the Lord, because He has dealt bountifully with me.

ONE

DAVE SISKO HEARD the dull thunk and the yelp of pain almost simultaneously. He shoved the handle of his hammer into his waistband and sprinted around the corner. The old wooden fence they were rebuilding as part of Harrison's annual Christmas-in-April project leaned in a dozen crazy directions and forced him to zigzag accordingly.

He pulled up at the sight of a slender young woman dressed in denim capris and a plain red T-shirt. Her straight, black hair was bundled into a long ponytail. She held the fingers of her left hand as she danced in place. Dave searched his memory for her name but came up short. This was the first day of the month-long project, and although he'd met all twelve of his volunteers this morning, it generally took him a day or so to sort them out in his head.

He took both of her hands in his. "You OK?"

She bounced on her toes. "No!"

Dave pried her fingers apart. "Let's take a look." He inspected her left hand and then her right. His gaze went to her face and back to her hands. He couldn't find a single mark on the delicate skin, and as far as he could tell her manicure was unscathed. He grinned at her. "I think you'll live."

She yanked her hands out of his and glared at him with eyes as brown as his morning coffee. "It hurts."

Dave couldn't be sure, but there might have been a murmured *Neanderthal* tacked to the end of her comment. He took off his cap, ran a hand through his sweaty hair, and prayed for God to deliver him from beautiful, prissy females. "I'm sorry. Remind me of your name?"

"Lisa Garcia."

"Come with me, Lisa." Dave led her away from the scene of the accident and through a gap in the boards. When they reached the porch of the old two-story house, he opened a large ice chest and pulled out a bottle of cold water. He held it up, and when she nodded he twisted the top free and handed it to her. Then he retrieved the first aid kit he always kept on hand. Stacks of gauze, rows of tape, a box of Band-Aids, a pair of scissors, and a bottle of aspirin. Everything handy and in order. He took out an emergency ice pack, gave it a quick twist, and shook it until he felt it growing cold. It wouldn't last long in the springtime Texas sun, but then there wasn't much of an injury to soothe.

Lisa was standing so close behind him, he could feel her breath on his neck. The sensation did funny things to his stomach. He turned and looked at her, his eyebrows raised.

She stepped back and motioned to the kit. "Just admiring. You could triage war victims from that." She held up a finger. "I cut myself a couple of days ago making a salad and never did find a Band-Aid, and I know I just bought a box last week."

"It pays to be prepared." He held out the ice pack. "Here you go."

"Thank you." Lisa sat on the steps, put her bottle on the porch, and held the cold pack to her fingers. "Much better." She patted the space beside her. "Take a break with me?"

Dave looked at the fence. The waiting work nagged at him, but he hated to be rude. *Five minutes.* He snagged a second bottle for himself and sat.

"It really does hurt."

"I believe you." He leaned back on his elbows. "I can assign you to something less dangerous if you like."

"The fence is fine."

He took a long drink from the bottle. "Is this your first project?"

She nodded and continued to nurse her invisible wound.

"You live in Harrison?"

Lisa snorted. "Unfortunately."

He crossed his ankles. "You don't like it?"

Lisa laid the ice pack aside, mirrored his pose, and stared into space. "This place is the pimple on the right butt cheek of Podunk towns."

"That's harsh."

"Not harsh enough most days," she said.

"How did you end up in a place you dislike so much?"

"It wasn't my idea. Mom has an old school friend here. We came for a visit after Dad died, and Mom decided she liked small-town life." Lisa sighed. "Mom's the spur-of-the-moment sort, more so now that she's on her own. I didn't like her decision, but I figured I could live with it for a few months...you know, until the wind blew one of us in a different direction. But six months later we're still here. She keeps telling me I'll get used to it, but I miss Los Angeles. Sorry if that insults you."

He shook his head. "I don't live in Harrison. I live across the bridge in Yellow Veil."

She turned her head a fraction and looked at him from the corner of her eye. "The pimple on the left." But she was smiling.

He swallowed a sudden lump in his throat. *Get a grip, Sisko.* "You work?"

She shook her head. "Not right now. Dad's insurance was substantial, so I'm taking some time off from school to see Mom settled. I'll have to make a decision before the fall, but for now...it feels nice to just go with the flow."

Dave nodded his approval, knowing full well that living like that would drive him crazy. He needed structure.

"What do you do in Yellow Veil?" she asked.

"Oh, I stay busy. I work, part time, in an insurance office."

"That sounds interesting."

"It has its moments, but my other job is where the action really is."

"And that is?"

"For now, I'm the youth pastor at Abundant Life Church."

"For now?"

"Well, no one's a youth pastor forever. It's a training ground."

Something hardened in her eyes. "What are you training for?"

"Full-time ministry. I'll pastor someday." He chuckled. "With a name like David Elijah Sisko, I figure that's a good thing."

Lisa scrambled to her feet. "I better get back to that fence."

Dave sat up. *What got into her?* "How's the hand?"

"Great." The word and the smile were tight.

"Are you OK?"

"Fine."

Dave got to his feet and watched her go, hands fisted on his hips. He could speak female with the best, and he knew that when a woman said she was *fine*, she was anything but.

LISA WENT BACK to work pulling the old boards from the framework of the fence. She got the occasional glimpse of Dave as the day wore on. He seemed to be everywhere, holding a ladder here, offering a quick piece of advice there, and passing out water to all as the temperature climbed. He did it all with a ready smile and a steady focus that made the recipient feel like they were the center of his universe for a few seconds.

She glanced at the invisible injury to her hand, convinced that she could still feel his hands on hers. Lisa was honest enough to admit to herself that she'd played that up a bit when he'd come to her rescue, taking full advantage of the opportunity to get to know their ruggedly handsome leader.

Another board came free with a screech of rusted nails, and Lisa saw Dave glance her way from under the brim of his worn baseball cap. For just a second, he studied her with those amazing blue eyes before he went back to work.

Lisa forced herself back to her job. Ignoring David Elijah Sisko wouldn't be easy, but Lisa planned to work at it because now she knew all there was to know. The very last thing she needed in her life right now was someone with aspirations to the ministry. Especially when that someone had a scruffy jawline, a mouth that begged kissing, and the power to unleash hordes of butterflies in her stomach.

She stacked the board with the others she'd liberated. *Not going there. Not today, not ever!* She straightened and wiped beads of perspiration from her forehead, grateful when a cloud blotted out the glare of the sun for a few seconds. Lisa looked up, addressing her Heavenly Father. *It's got nothing to do with You, Father. You know I love You, but...* She closed her eyes and remembered another earnest face and charismatic personality. *Fool me once, shame on you, fool me twice, shame on me.*

"OK everyone," Dave called from the front of the house. "Let's wrap it up for today. Can I get everyone over here for a second? We need to talk about next week."

Lisa followed the rest of the volunteers to the porch. Dave stood next to the rail, a tray piled high with some kind of goodies in one hand, his free arm around the shoulders of a slight, elderly woman.

"I want you all to meet Mrs. Craig."

Mrs. Craig raised a shaky hand and nodded to the group gathered around the steps. Dave turned her and led her to a weathered rocker with a faded plaid cushion. Once she was seated, he returned to his spot on the porch and hefted the tray. "While you guys were working, Mrs. Craig baked us a batch of sugar cookies." He plucked one from the tray and bit off a healthy chunk. "They're awesome." Dave handed the tray to the nearest volunteer. "Pass those around, would you?" He straightened. "You guys have done a terrific job today, and I appreciate your hard work. We'll meet again next Saturday morning at eight."

The girl on Lisa's left leaned in and whispered in her ear. "Isn't he just the cutest thing? That was a pretty smooth trick you pulled with the hammer this morning. I have a turned ankle planned for next week." The girl sighed, her gaze following Dave as he moved around on the porch. "I mean really, Hubba...hubba."

Heat flushed Lisa's cheeks. "I...you...what...?" She turned away, embarrassed because it was partly true, ashamed at the sudden urge to stomp on the girl's toes, and jealous at the idea of Dave's hands on Miss *Hubba's* ankle.

How dare she...? Lisa swallowed and wrapped herself in indifference. She looked at the guy she couldn't afford to like and leaned over to return the whisper. "Preacher boy? Honey, he's all yours." She watched Dave interact with a few of his straggling flock of volunteers, cringing when his infectious laugh rang from the porch, lifting the tiny hairs on the back of her neck with an emotion she refused to name.

Lisa turned in her tools and hurried to her car. She stopped when a pitiful cry reached her ears. When it came a second time— from somewhere beneath her car—she stooped to investigate.

"Oh..." Sitting next to one of her rear tires, in a position that would surely have gotten it squished, was a tiny white kitten. Lisa scooped it up, leaned against her bumper, and lifted the scrap of fur to her face. "Where did you come from?" If she were any judge, the kitty was only a few weeks old. She looked up and down the street. Surely there was a mother cat searching for her baby.

"What do you have there?"

Lisa started at the question, so preoccupied with her find she hadn't heard Dave's approach. She held the kitten out so he could see. "Poor baby was under my car."

Dave touched a finger to the tiny fur-covered head and stroked it down the feline back. "Cute."

"Do you think it belongs to Mrs. Craig?"

"I don't think so. She mentioned being allergic to cats when we visited last week."

"Hmm..." Lisa took another look up the street, scooted past Dave, and opened her car door.

"What are you doing?"

"I guess I just became a cat owner."

"What? You can't make a decision like that on the spur of the moment. You don't have food, you don't have a litter box—"

"Last time I checked, there was a grocery store on my way home."

"Lisa, you don't even know if it's weaned."

"What would you have me do? I can't just leave it on the street."

He held out his hand. "Let me have it. Yellow Veil has a shelter with an emergency drop off—"

Lisa bristled at his words, angling the kitten out of his reach. "Back off. I don't need you to make decisions for me."

He took a step back and ran a hand through his hair. "Sorry, that came out wrong. All I meant was that pets are a big responsibility. You aren't prepared. You're not even sure you're staying in town."

Lisa examined the cat.

"What are you looking for?"

"An umbilical cord that ties this animal to Harrison."

"That's not funny."

"Neither was your suggestion to dump it at the pound."

They glared at each other for several seconds. Dave lost the stare down. He raised both hands in a gesture of surrender. "Have fun with your new charge. I'll see you next week."

"Don't count on it." Lisa slid into her seat, slammed the door, and left Dave Sisko in the dust of her departure.

TWO

LISA SHIFTED the bag of groceries from one hip to the other and knocked on her mom's front door. After several moments, she boosted herself up on her toes and tried to peer through the tiny window that decorated the top of the door.

"Mom?"

She rolled her eyes, put the sack on the porch, and tried the knob. Locked. Lisa huffed and dug her keys out of her pocket. She pushed open the door, leaned in, and looked around the cluttered living room. "Mom, I picked up your groceries." No response.

Lisa collected the bag, stepped over a stack of magazines, detoured around a table laden with quilting supplies, and entered the kitchen. It too was empty. She put the bag on the cluttered bar, knocking a stack of mail to the floor in the process. As she stooped to retrieve the envelopes, Lisa pulled out her cell phone and found the message her mother had sent earlier.

Swamped here. Could you run by the store for me? List to follow.

The list was short, and since Lisa had needed to shop for the kitten, she'd been glad to oblige. But where had Mom gone?

She crossed to the door leading out to the garage. Mom's car was MIA. Lisa smirked. *She probably went to the store to get the things she sent me after.* She dialed her mother's number, not the least surprised when the ringtone sounded from somewhere in the living room. *Oh, well.* She put the milk and lettuce in the fridge, left the rest in the bag for her mother to deal with, and retraced her steps to the front door. She needed to get the kitten settled and fix something for both of them to eat. Her phone rang before she reached her mom's front door.

A glance at the screen made her smile. She swiped the call open. "Hey, Jemma."

"What's going on?"

"Not much. I brought some stuff over to Moms. Thought I might beg dinner, but she isn't here. Guess I'll go home and heat up a can of soup."

"All the way home?"

Lisa grinned. When Mom made the decision to stay in Harrison, she'd bought a duplex. She lived in one half, Lisa in the other. "Hey, a lot could happen between her door and mine. I could stub my toe or get a mosquito bite."

"Wimp." Jemma chuckled. "In the mood for a better offer?"

"Such as..."

"Thought about trying out Harrison's new restaurant. You want to come?"

"Harrison has a new restaurant?" *Probably some barbeque place.* Lisa grimaced. She disliked the sweet red sauce that Texan's insisted on pouring over every cut of meat. "I don't—"

"It's Sushi..."

Lisa stopped. "Sushi...in Harrison? This I have to see. I don't promise I'll eat it, but I have to see it."

Jemma's laughter rang in her ears. "I'm right there with you, but I have to check it out. Thirty minutes?"

"Sure." Lisa remembered the kitten. "On second thought, I'm gonna need an hour."

DAVE DROVE BACK to Yellow Veil, turning his confrontation with the lovely Lisa Garcia over and over in his mind. She'd gotten a little weird after he'd patched up her finger, but that was nothing compared to the cat thing.

He'd only been trying to help. You didn't just pick up a stray animal and take it home. He liked animals, but before he'd adopted a pet he'd spent weeks reading and researching breeds and temperament.

But you're not regular people. Dave acknowledged that with a shrug. He knew his desire for neatness and structure could put some people off. The majority of the people he interacted with did not share the a-place-for-everything-and-everything-in-its-place mindset he'd left the orphanage with. But after five years of living on his own, the control issues bred by his institutional upbringing were beginning to lessen. At least he'd thought so until today.

Now, his idiosyncrasies had caused one of his volunteers to bail on him after only a day. That was a shame. There was something... mesmerizing about Lisa Garcia and Dave would have enjoyed the chance to know her better.

He pushed Lisa to the back of his mind as he turned off the blacktop onto the dirt road that led to his house. It struck him, as it always did, that if you didn't know what lay at the end of the road, you'd dismiss the property as worthless. But Dave knew better.

Despite the layer of dirt that coated his truck after every trip up and down the road, despite the swamp the drive became when it rained, despite the way those things clashed with his nearly OCD personality, the rented house that sat in the middle of the three lush acres had become his home.

At the base of the hill he turned a final corner and grinned. Chester, the black lab his research had netted him, crouched in the grass along the side of the road. The dog had an ear for the sound of the old pickup and never failed to be waiting. Dave honked, and the race to the end of the road was on. Chester sprinted for home, a mere three-tenths of a mile away, tongue out, legs pumping. Dave eased down on the gas pedal, kicking up dust as he gave the dog a run for his money. As always, Chester beat him. The dog didn't have to slow down to take the sharp turn into the drive.

Chester waited for Dave to open his door before rushing over with his toothy dog-grin. Dave laughed at the victory he saw in the dog's eyes. He stooped to rub the black head, clasping both ears in his hands and tugging. "Beat me again, didn't you?" Chester's response was a tail wag that shook his whole body.

Dave gave the dog a playful shove, unlocked the door to his workshop, and began to unload his tools. Each item received a thorough inspection and wipe-down before being placed in the exact spot he'd removed it from that morning. Once the shop was re-organized to his liking, he headed to his house. Inside, he hung his keys on the hook by the door, toed off his tennis shoes, and lined them up next to his boots. He noticed that the rug in the entry was a bit crooked and bent to straighten it. Then stopped. He stared at the rug. His fingers itched to make it rest perfectly parallel to the door. He walked away just to prove that he could.

———

LISA STARED AT THEIR PLATES. Jemma's Lucky Lady roll was a little lopsided, but her own Crunchy Crab looked pretty good. The avocado was the perfect shade of green, and the crab meat looked juicy and tender.

"Meet your L.A. expectations?" Jemma asked.

"Visually."

Jemma twisted her plate this way and that, her expression doubtful. "I know this was my idea, but...I think this needs some serious blessing before I can eat it."

Lisa laughed. "It isn't raw, you know."

"Yeah, well." Jemma bowed her head and muttered a quick grace. "Better safe than sorry," she said when she straightened.

Lisa moved half of the crab roll to Jemma's plate and accepted half of the Lucky Lady in return. "Try it before you decide." She motioned to the center of the table and the remains of their appetizer. "There's always the crab rangoon if this doesn't work out." She picked up her chopsticks and lifted a small bite to her mouth. Jemma's gaze followed the action expectantly.

She chewed thoughtfully, comparing this to the L.A. offerings she missed so much. *Oh my...* She swallowed and grinned across the table. "It's really good."

Jemma picked up her fork, cut into a slice of the Lucky Lady, closed her eyes, and popped it in her mouth.

Lisa watched as her friend's eyebrows rose. Jemma's eyes opened, and she looked at her plate.

"Oh man...sushi, where have you been all my life?" She cut a piece of the Crunchy Crab and forked it up, motioning to Lisa's chopsticks. "We're going to come here...a lot. You're going to have to teach me how to use those. I don't want to look like a rookie."

They ate in silence for a few minutes, Lisa enjoying a treat she hadn't had in the six months since moving to Harrison. Jemma was totally wrapped up in the tastes and textures of something new.

When Jemma forked up her last bite of sushi and the crab rangoon was nothing but a shared memory, she waved at the placard sitting on the back of the table. "Talk to me about dessert. The almond biscuit, rice pudding, and egg tart are pretty self-explanatory, but what is *Tong Sui*?"

Lisa studied the picture. "It's sort of a warm, sweet soup. There are lots of variations, but this one looks like a thin custard." She pointed to another picture. "I'm having the rice pudding."

"I think I'll try the *Tong Sui*. I might as well go for the whole experience."

While they waited for their desserts Lisa leaned back in her chair. "What did you do today?"

"We had softball practice, and I've gotta tell you, I'm pumped. We have a great team of kids this year. After that I went home and worked on my message for youth group tomorrow. You?"

"I worked with one of the groups doing a Christmas-in-April project, and I adopted a kitten."

"I think you get the prize for most interesting day. You didn't tell me you were thinking about doing the Christmas-in-April thing."

"Oh, you know me. It was an impulse. I didn't really decide until last night, didn't know if they'd take a last-minute volunteer." Lisa studied her friend. Jemma was Praise Tabernacle's youth pastor. Dave held that spot in Harrison. Did they know each other? As much as she didn't really want to know Dave any better, there was something compelling about him. "I...um...met someone you might know. Dave Sisko?"

Jemma sat back as their dessert was placed on the table. She eyed hers for a second before picking up her spoon. "David Elijah Sisko. Hunk city and a very strange bird."

Lisa frowned, still more than a little angry over their final confrontation. "Agree to the first. The man is serious eye candy. And strange?" She related the story of the cat. "I didn't appreciate his interference."

"You'll have to know some of Dave's history to appreciate him."

"I don't want to appreciate him, and I don't need gossip."

Jemma brushed her objections aside. "Everything I'm going to tell you is common knowledge." She paused, obviously ordering her thoughts. Her eyes came back to Lisa's with a question. "Do you know what God's will for your life is?"

"I wish. I'm looking, I'm praying, but..." She lifted her hands in surrender. "That's the only good part about this move. It gave me an excuse to take time away from college and the endless search for my niche in the world. I'll be twenty-two in October. Maybe God will answer that prayer for my birthday." She spooned up a bite of her pudding. "What does my future have to do with understanding Dave?"

"Just drawing a comparison. You're still looking, but Dave says he's known that God intended him for the ministry all his life. Called from his mother's womb—my words, not his. He'd never use that phrase since he never knew his mother."

"He—"

"He was raised in an orphanage."

Some of Lisa's irritation faded. "That's awful."

"You'd think so, wouldn't you? But instead, it's almost as if Dave is God's own personal example of the lemon-lemonade cliché. Don't get me wrong, he's got quirks. He's obsessively neat, organized to a fault, and thinks others should be the same."

The cat thing began to make sense. The spontaneous decision to take the kitten home probably made him crazy.

"He can be a bit of a pain, but on the flip side, he loves the kids in his youth group with a dedication you don't find in a lot of twenty-three-year-olds these days. He's funny, he's smart, and he lives a life of service because he wants to follow Christ's example." Jemma pushed her empty bowl aside and studied Lisa with a sly smile. "You got your eye on Yellow Veil's most eligible bachelor?"

Lisa snorted. "Please. We did not enjoy each other's company. Besides, you and I have had this talk. You can recite my history almost as well as you can Dave's. There's no aspiring minister in my romantic future."

THREE

"ALL RIGHT!" Lisa tossed the masking tape into the pile of painting supplies, ripped the bandana off her head, and let it lie where it fell. "Good grief." She waded through bags of painting supplies, crumpled newspapers she planned to use to protect the wood floors, and muttered under her breath all the way to her bedroom Saturday morning. "It's not like I don't have plenty of projects of my own to work on." She'd not made the decision to stay in Harrison beyond the summer, but she was living in the duplex rent free. The least she could do, while she waited for a plan, was make a few simple upgrades. That way, if she stayed, she had a decent place to live, and if she moved on, Mom could charge a higher rent to future tenants.

You made a commitment.

Lisa frowned at the voice of her conscience. This is what being raised in a preacher's house got you. A moral compass that fought against every little infraction. She looked heavenward. "I really, really do not want to spend the day in the company of Dave Sisko."

Silence was her only answer.

Lisa hunted up Snowflake, settled the kitten in the bathroom with food, water, and the litter box, closed the door, then grabbed her keys. She stomped to her car. Her mood had vacillated all week long. One moment, she was willing to let bygones be bygones where Dave was concerned and even felt a bit giddy at the thought of seeing him again. The next moment, she was filled with resolve, determined to avoid the handsome preacher, knowing that those feelings of anticipation were stupid and likely to get her into more trouble than she wanted to deal with.

But he was just so stinking cute, and the things Jemma had shared made him even more attractive. She felt a little sorry for him as well. Her frustrated breath echoed in the car. Dad had been MIA for ninety percent of her life, but she knew who he was. She could accept that he loved her even if he hadn't seemed to know how to show it. And she'd always had Mom.

And she'd always had a home. They'd bounced around a lot, never in one place more than four or five years. But she'd always had her own room, her space, her place. A dinner table with at least one loving adult ready to discuss her day and help with her home-work, someone to listen to her dreams for the future. To grow up without those things...Lisa could only imagine how hard that would be and the scars it would leave behind.

When she tried to imagine life in an orphanage, she pictured a big room with a dozen beds divided by tiny, cramped dressers. Kids standing in line with a tray to get a tasteless meal. Homework done at a solitary desk. Dreams whispered in a dark room with no one to listen. Mostly she pictured a little boy with no one to love him... ever... and it tugged at her heart. And her heart, aching with sympathy for Dave—a man who was the opposite of everything she was determined to have out of life—was a dangerous thing.

And now? Well, now she was going to be late, and instead of blending in with the others, doing her job, and ignoring Dave, she'd be forced to speak to him...one-on-one...while looking into those gorgeous blue eyes.

———

DAVE FROWNED over his clipboard as his group of volunteers

swarmed, like locusts in a wheat field, over the two dozen donuts he'd brought. His shoulders slumped when the count came up one short. He'd hoped...well, his hopes had never had much bearing on reality. Fretting over Lisa's absence wouldn't get the fence rebuilt or the outside of the house scraped.

"Guys! Listen up." He called the group to order, and they lined up at the foot of the porch, faces eager, ready to get to work, tools slung at their sides like weapons. It reminded him of Nehemiah 4:6. *So built we the wall; and all the wall was joined together unto the half thereof: for the people had a mind to work.* Dave grinned. That ratty fence didn't stand a chance.

"OK. Our two projects for the day are rebuilding the fence and getting the outside of the house prepared for a fresh coat of paint." He called off three names and motioned to the neat stacks of lumber next to the drive. "You guys get started on the fence. Everyone else, pick a side of the house, and start scraping off that old paint. There's a ladder on each side of the house. Use the buddy system when you need to climb. We'll switch around a bit after lunch. I'm taking fence-duty for now. Remember your fluids, there's sunscreen on the porch if you need some, and there are a few extra tools in the back of my truck. Give a yell if you need anything."

They scattered to their jobs like soldiers moving to battle stations. Dave took a walk around the house to make sure everyone wore gloves and goggles. He didn't need bloody knuckles or paint chips in eyes to slow them down. Mostly he wanted to make sure that for every one on a ladder, there was a person below ready to offer assistance. Satisfied, he crossed to his truck. He'd hidden his favorite hammer under the seat in the cab. He reached in and felt around, then stretched in further. It must have shifted while he was driving. His fingers brushed the satin finish of the wooden handle. *There you are.*

"Sorry I'm late."

Dave jerked at the words and smacked his head on the steering wheel. "Ouch!" He straightened, his hammer in one hand, the other rubbing the tender spot, a frown focused on the newcomer.

"Sorry...again," Lisa said. "You aren't bleeding or anything, are you?"

Dave ignored the question and took in Lisa's paint-splattered jeans and shirt. She was late, but at least she'd come prepared to work. "I thought you weren't..." He trailed off when her eyes narrowed slightly. *You wanted a chance to know this woman better. Are you going to remind her of your disagreement, or be thankful she's here?* "No problem," he amended. "We're just getting started." He motioned to her clothes. "But we aren't painting today."

"Oh." Lisa glanced down at her clothes. When she looked back up, she wore an easy smile. "I'm doing some remodeling at home too. I was painting and lost track of the time."

Dave nodded. "Perfect. Ready to get back to the fence?"

At her answering nod, he took her arm and led her to the back of the truck. There was one hammer left. He handed it to her, along with a pair of gloves, and motioned to the activity in the yard. "Just pick a spot. Did you eat? I think there are some donuts left on the porch."

"Thanks." She hefted the hammer as if checking the weight and balance and stuffed the gloves in her back pocket. "I never turn down sweets. I'll check that out before I get to work."

He watched her go. She seemed fine this morning. Maybe he'd blown the whole thing out of proportion. He shrugged it away, his mind moving ahead to the end of the day. She was remodeling. He might be able to leverage that into an opportunity to spend some time with her. He could offer to lend a hand. And if she said yes, they had to eat. Dave rested his hammer on his shoulder and walked to the fence line with a lighter heart than he'd had all week.

―――――

"OK GUYS. Let's call it a day."

Lisa stepped back from the house at Dave's words, dropped the scraper to the ground, and shook off the heavy gloves. She pulled at her sweaty clothes, dislodging a small cloud of dust and paint chips. Fence repair this morning, paint removal all afternoon. Exhaustion was too light a word for what she was feeling. Every muscle and bone in her body ached. All she wanted was a large cheese Coney with onion rings, a hot shower, and a soft mattress, in that order. *But wait!* She had two rooms of her own to paint once she got home. The thought brought slumped shoulders and a soft whimper.

The rest of the group was moving to the front yard, and Lisa followed, her spirit dragging right along with her feet. She moved to the edge of the porch and sank to the grass. At this point, it was sit or fall. She looked up at Dave as he directed his incredible smile toward the volunteers.

"You guys are the best," he said. "We're at least a half a day ahead of schedule. Go home and get some rest tonight. You've earned it. We'll meet back here next Saturday morning. We'll get busy painting the outside of the house and put some wood sealer on that fence."

The group shuffled away with tired high-fives and thumbs up. When a pair of frayed jeans and worn tennis shoes stepped next to her, Lisa let her gaze drift up. "Hey, Dave."

He squatted beside her. "You OK?"

She shook her head. "After careful consideration, I don't think I can stand." She managed to straighten her legs, but instead of getting to her feet, she leaned back in the grass. "You can leave me here, I'll be fine."

"Do you want me to go borrow a quilt from Mrs. Craig? The nights can still be a little chilly."

"No, that's fine. I'll be dead before morning."

Dave laughed, stood, and held out a hand. "Come on."

Lisa took the hand and allowed him to pull her to her feet. She groaned as over worked muscles took her weight. "Oh, my goodness." She closed her eyes and willed the throbbing away. "I'm not a slouch. How can I be so sore?"

"Different muscle groups, probably," Dave answered. "A warm bath'll help."

"Yeah. That's on my list. After dinner and after I do some painting of my own."

Dave grinned. "You want some help with that?"

Lisa took a step back and crossed her arms, grinning when his ears turned cherry red.

"With the painting, I mean." His expression was hopeful, but her heart was flashing a yellow danger sign. "I don't think—"

"I'm sorry about last week. I was out of line with the kitten thing. I'd like a chance to make it up to you."

Lisa lifted a hand. "It's not that. You worked harder than any two of us put together today. You need to go home as much as I do. I only have two rooms to do tonight. It'll take a couple of hours. I'll be fine."

"If you let me help, it'll just take an hour. Think about that. Sixty minutes closer to that hot bath. I'll even swing by Sonic and grab some dinner."

The picture his words painted was almost enough to make her weep in anticipation. She took a deep breath. Involvement with Dave Sisko was taboo on more levels than she could count. *And aren't you special? What reason have you got to think he's offering anything other than friendship?* She conceded the point to the annoying little voice in her head. He was probably just lonely. She'd had guy friends before. She could like Dave without *liking* him. Lisa held out her hand. "You've got yourself a deal. Foot-long Coney, large onion rings."

"Chocolate shake?"

"You really know how to sweet-talk a woman, don't you?"

Dave grinned. "It's a gift."

FOUR

DAVE MOUNTED the steps on the left half of the wide porch that fronted the duplex. The place was tidy and neat, red brick with black shutters on all the windows. Windows that were currently devoid of light. He juggled two sacks of food and a drink carrier. Not finding a doorbell, he gently kicked the bottom of the storm door. "Lisa." He waited a few moments before increasing the force of the kicks. Nothing.

He turned in a complete circle and noticed for the first time that her car wasn't in the drive. *How did I stop at Sonic and beat her back here?* Dave glanced around with a frustrated sigh, looking for someplace other than the floor of the porch to set the food. In the quickly gathering dusk he spotted an old wooden swing on the other side of the deck. He crossed the creaking boards, set the bags in the swing and pulled his phone from his pocket. He opened the note he'd made of her address and compared it to the house number. He had the right place. What could she... He turned when headlights swept across him and watched Lisa's car pull into the driveway.

She waved at him as she got out. "Sorry, small change in plans." She ducked back into the car, emerged with sacks, and held them up. "I got Mexican."

Dave frowned at her and motioned to the swing. "I thought you wanted a Coney."

Lisa came up the steps. "I know. But I passed some guy selling tacos out of a vending trailer out on the highway. Had my mouth watering so bad I almost drooled on myself. I had to stop. I'd have called you, but I didn't have your number. Don't worry, I bought enough to share." She dumped the bags into his arms and turned to unlock the door. "Who knows? Tacos with onion rings and chocolate shakes just may be the next great food sensation." Lisa nudged the door open with her foot, turned back for the bags, and jerked her head in the direction of the door. "Grab the shakes and come on in. I'm starving."

She swished through the door like a tornado on the open prairie, leaving Dave blinking in her wake. He turned to retrieve the sonic bags. How could she send him for food, then stop to buy food on her way home? Did she really expect him to be good with that? Dave didn't know what to think or do. The idea of combining chocolate shakes with roach coach tacos came close to turning his stomach.

"You coming?"

Dave looked up to see Lisa leaning out the door and smiling.

"Umm...sure." He followed her into the house and hesitated in the doorway, dismayed. Unpacked boxes were stacked in the middle of the room. The bare wall opposite the front door was covered in random strokes of paint in various colors. It looked a bit like a four-year-old had been turned loose with finger paints. Old newspapers covered the floor, and more lay in piles around the room next to cans and brushes. He swallowed and rolled his head on his shoulders at the sudden itch that formed between his shoulder blades. There was no furniture in the room save a paint-stained coffee table, two lawn chairs, and a flat-screen TV sitting on a stand made out of stacked milk crates.

Lisa motioned to the low table. "Just put the food there. I'll get some paper plates and napkins. Sorry about the mess." She called over her shoulder, "Like I said, I'm painting and working on the floors. And since I haven't decided if I'm staying beyond the summer, there wasn't much point in buying a bunch of furniture or unpacking my stuff."

He stared at the thick layer of dust on the table she'd indicated. "Better bring a damp rag too."

"For?"

Seriously? "You could plant a garden on this table." He did his best to keep his comment light, but the mess of this room made his skin crawl. The house wasn't dirty, just in total disarray. *How does she live like this?* This would...was...driving him crazy. *Buck up, Sisko. You can deal with this.*

Lisa came back into the room, gave the table a cursory swipe, and started setting food out on plates and napkins. She pulled one of the lawn chairs close to the table and sat, motioning to the other. "Help yourself."

Dave did as instructed. He handed Lisa a shake and watched her take a healthy slurp on the heels of a taco oozing with salsa and guacamole.

"That's pretty good." She unwrapped a second and motioned to the stack. "Better hurry. You're almost two behind."

Dave blew out a breath and fished his cheeseburger out of the bag. He spread the wrapper on the table, smoothing the wrinkles as best he could before laying his order of onion rings on the paper. "I think I'll stick with this, thanks." As hungry as he was, the chaos in the room was overriding his appetite. If he didn't get out of here, he'd start cleaning her house, and he didn't think that would earn him any points. He bowed his head and focused on his food. *Father, I really like this girl and I don't want to blow it. Please give me strength.*

"I'm sorry," Lisa whispered.

He looked up. "What?"

"You were so sweet, offering to buy my dinner, and I totally messed that up." She picked at the breading on an onion ring. Small golden crumbs fell to the table.

Dave stared at them, itching to rake them into a neat pile, to dispose of them.

Lisa continued. "I have a really bad habit of acting before I think things through. I didn't mean to hurt your feelings. Forgive me?"

Dave forced his gaze from the crumbs and found himself staring into her expressive brown eyes. He could get lost there. If he concentrated his attention there, maybe he could beat back the impulses begging him to take some action. "It's OK."

"Really? Because you had such a serious frown on your face."

"Oh, I was trying to think of the best way to tell you how beautiful you are."

Her response was a dazzling smile. "Nice save."

Dave grinned in return, and the demons pressing at his consciousness retreated a step. He pried his gaze from hers and looked at the burger in his hands. *Just breathe and eat.* He took a healthy bite. "Where's the kitten?"

"I left her in the bathroom this morning. I won't give her unsupervised run of the house until I'm sure she's good with the litter box."

"How's that going?"

"So far so good. I'll check on her after we eat, but since we're painting, I'll leave her in there for now."

"Probably for the best." He motioned around the room while he chewed. He swallowed and said, "You've got quite a...mess... happening here. Tell me what you're doing to the place."

"Floors and walls for now. All of the rooms had some minor sheetrock damage that needed fixing. I did that yesterday." She swiped at the remaining dust on the table. "That's where this came from. Once I get the painting done throughout, I'll tackle the floors."

"Carpet?" he asked.

"Are you kidding me?" She kicked some of the newspaper aside and tapped the exposed wood with her foot. "This is real wood, that's why I'm trying to keep it covered. I'll strip it and give it some new varnish. It'll be beautiful."

Dave looked around, nodding in agreement. "I can see it." He wiped a smudge of ketchup from the corner of his mouth. "You're pretty handy for a girl."

LISA SAT BACK and stared at him. *Sexist, full-of-himself jerk.* She pointed a half-eaten onion ring in his direction. When she spoke, her voice carried the twang of an artificial Southern accent. "Oh, don't you worry none, sugar. I can cook, clean, and rear the chillen' with the rest of the women folk." She straightened, her voice returning to normal. "But I enjoy working with my hands, and I can comprehend a tutorial video on YouTube just fine, thank you very much." She leaned forward and swept the trash from their dinner into an empty bag.

Dave placed a hand on hers, and she looked up. Electricity zapped up her arm, leaving her fingers tingling in the aftermath. Lisa jerked her hand free and focused on her chore.

"I'm sorry," Dave said. "I guess I was thinking about last week's girly girl with the injured thumb." He stood and stepped into her space until she had no choice but to look at him. "If you'll forgive me, we can be even."

Lisa averted her eyes as heat flooded her cheeks at the reminder of her manufactured meet-the-hunk injury. *That was before I found out he was a preacher.* Another reminder, but this one straightened her back. "I'm good with even," she told him, all business. "We better get a move on if we want to get those two rooms painted."

Dave took the trash bag from her hands. "Why don't you go check on the kitten—"

"Snowflake."

"Nice, and sort out what needs to be done while I clean up this mess? When I'm finished, you can show me what you want me to do."

She blinked at him. Cleaning was never at the top of her

list. "Sure."

Dave went one way and Lisa the other. She peeked into the bathroom. Snowflake was asleep on the rug. The litter box showed signs of use. "Good girl," she whispered. She eased the door shut, stood in the hall, and studied the rooms on either side. Her bedroom and the spare. Her room held a bed and more boxes. She wasn't sure what the spare would be just yet. She had lots of things in storage—books, an elliptical, a daybed she'd picked up at a recent yard sale. She had tons of options. What she didn't have was a decision about her future in Harrison.

The paint for the spare was a robin's egg blue, and for her room she'd settled on a pale yellow. There would be no impersonal white or boring beige in her home. Lisa decided to give Dave the blue room. She wanted the satisfaction of sprucing up her own space.

She returned to the living room and stopped in her tracks. The dinner mess was more than cleared away. The table was wiped to a shine. The lawn chairs were positioned neatly in front of the television. And unless she was mistaken, the newspapers taped to the floor had been swept, because there wasn't an onion ring crumb in sight. She frowned, then recalled Jemma's comment about Dave being a bit OCD. The memory also explained Dave's reaction to the tacos. He'd covered it well, but the impulse purchase had bothered him. She probably should have resisted the urge, but spontaneity kept her life interesting.

Between her tacos and his cleaning, Lisa figured they were about even on the annoyance scale, with the indicator hovering somewhere in the middle, between zero and extreme. She brushed the visual aside. If they were going to be friends, allowances would need to be made on both sides.

Dave came into the room, drying his hands on a towel. "Are we ready?"

"Yeah." She motioned to the room. "Looks good."

He ducked his head. "Oh, you know...a job worth doing..."

"Is worth doing well." Lisa finished the cliché and motioned for him to follow. "Let's see how good you are at painting."

FIVE

He was pretty good Lisa mused as she rolled yellow paint over the walls of her room. And even with the caution lights blinking fast and furious in her heart, she had to admit that he was nice to have around. The rooms they worked in were directly opposite each other, and with the doors wide open their get-to-know-each-other conversation flowed as easily as the paint.

"Tell me about yourself," Dave said.

"I can't tell you how much I hate that question." Lisa pulled masking tape from the edges of a window and frowned. As careful as she'd been, there were still a few spots where the yellow paint stained the white of the old fashioned window casing. *Drat!*

"Why's that?"

"It's just so open-ended. You say too much, and people think you're blathering. Say too little, and people think you've got something to hide." She concentrated on the wall around the closet door, doing her best not to make the same mess she'd made around the window. Dave's chuckle carried clearly from the other room.

"OK, direct questions then. Just remember that you asked for it when it begins to feel like an inquisition. How old are you?"

"Twenty-one."

"Birthday?"

"One a year."

"Lisa..."

She giggled. "October twelfth. You?"

"I'm an old man compared to you. I'll be twenty-four first of next month."

"Oh, wow," Lisa said. "What's your favorite color tennis ball?"

"Excuse me?"

He sounded puzzled, and Lisa grinned. "You know...for the legs of your walker."

"Very funny. You have siblings?"

"It's just me and Mom," she said.

"And you guys came to Harrison after your Dad died." It was a statement, not a question. He continued before she could reply. "School?"

"I'm almost done with my degree. Dad got sick, and I came home to help Mom manage, then we moved here. I'm still figuring out what comes next." She stooped to roll up more paint on the roller. This was where she put a stop to Dave's questions. He was inching too close to family details she had no intention of sharing. "And there you have it. End of story."

"Oh, I think there's much more to the story of Lisa Garcia than that."

Lisa whirled around, the paint roller held in front of her like a weapon. Yellow paint spattered the newspaper at her feet in a wide arc. She narrowed her eyes at the sight of Dave leaning against the door frame. "What are you doing?"

"I didn't mean to scare you. I finished and figured I'd help in here."

Lisa looked from him to the half painted room she stood in. "You finished the whole room?"

"Yes."

She studied him up and down, then compared her clothes to his. She was a yellow freckled mess. She didn't see a smidge of blue on him. She twirled her finger in a circle. He laughed out loud but

did a three-sixty in the doorway. Other than a few...very few...
traces of the day's grime, he was spotless.

His blue eyes met hers, and he shrugged. "I'm neat by nature.
Too neat sometimes. Just fair warning should my compulsions
annoy you down the road." He stepped into the room and surveyed
her progress. "This is nice. I like this color it's...peaceful." He
tisked, pulled a rag from his back pocket, crossed to the window,
and began wiping at the yellow smudges on the frame.

"I was going to do that."

"But if I do it while you finish the walls, we'll be done that
much sooner."

Unable to argue with his logic, Lisa returned to her chore. "So,
tell me about Dave Sisko. What makes a person a neatnik?"

"An institutional upbringing," he said without hesitation.

The roller in Lisa's hand paused mid-stroke. "I had dinner with
Jemma Hudson the other night. And...we weren't gossiping, just
indulging in some girl talk—"

"There's a difference?"

She glared at him over her shoulder. "Funny. Anyway, she
mentioned that you grew up in an orphanage. That made you
compulsive?"

"Mostly." There was a pause. She resisted the urge to turn and
watch him consider his answer. "I think it's hard for people to
understand. In that environment, you have less supervision than I
imagine you would in a house with a couple of parents. Some
people think that gives you more freedom, but the opposite is true.
Everything is very regimented. You get up, go to bed, and eat at the
same times each day, you bathe when it's your turn, you keep your
things put away or they become someone else's. For me, being neat
and organized was the only control I had over my life. Lifetime
habits are hard to break, but I'm working on it, right now in fact."

"How's that?"

"Hanging out with you," he said with a grin. "Your lack of
constraint is good for me."

"Spontaneity is my middle name." She gave a light patch a final swipe. "All done."

Dave came to stand beside her. "Looks great," he said. "Hold still a second." He leaned in and used the corner of the towel on her face.

He was so close, his eyes so intense, Lisa found it hard to breathe. She took a step back and batted at his hand.

"You've got paint—"

"Everywhere," Lisa finished. She took another step away and surveyed the room. "But it was worth it."

Dave nodded. "We make a good team."

Lisa shook away the warmth of his words. "Well, this part of the team is worn out." She motioned to the door. "Cold tea in the kitchen, then you have to go."

"Why don't you go ahead? I'll join you after I pick up all this paper."

"I'll do it tomorrow."

He shooed her toward the door. "You'll sleep better in a neat room."

She paused in the doorway and watched him bundle up the paper. "This really bugs you, doesn't it?"

Dave ducked his head. "It's making me a little crazy."

DAVE ENTERED the kitchen a few minutes later. Lisa had her back to him while she stood on her tiptoes and reached into a tall cupboard for the glasses. The bottom of her shirt separated from the waistband of her jeans, revealing the lines of a trim, and momentarily bare, waist.

His mouth turned to cotton, and he closed his eyes in an attempt to regain his sanity. A deep breath settled him, and he rustled the paper just to make some noise and keep from startling her. "Trash bag?" he asked when she turned his way.

"Oh sure." Lisa set the glasses on the counter, opened the cabinet under the sink, and bent to get a fresh bag.

The sight of the soft denim covering those curves was more disquieting than... Dave averted his eyes.

"Here you go." Lisa shook the bag open and held it out so that he could stuff the paper inside.

He couldn't make his feet move.

"Dave?"

Get a grip, Sisko. Dave shook himself free from whatever emotion held him captive and stepped forward. "Sorry, the day must be catching up with me."

"As much as I appreciate the help, you probably should have gone straight home." She picked up the glasses and nodded to the bar surrounding the small kitchen island. "Have a seat, drink your tea, and hit the road."

Dave pulled out one of the barstools for Lisa and waited until she was settled before seating himself. His hand brushed her shoulder in the process, and he marveled that she seemed oblivious to the electricity that sparked between them. He looked around the room, desperate to find a mundane topic for conversation. Otherwise it was just a matter of time before he fell at her feet and expressed his undying love.

Love?

He gulped his tea, choked, and spent the next thirty seconds trying to clear his windpipe. The fit of coughing expelled the thought and the liquid. It was the first time he'd ever been grateful for a near death experience. Lisa reached to pat his back and he stopped her with an upraised hand. The additional contact might finish the job the mis-swallowed tea started. "I'm good."

Back under control, he sat up with a deep breath, determined to focus on something other than Lisa. "I meant to tell you earlier, this is a great room."

He watched Lisa's gaze sweep the kitchen. "They did a good job on it."

"They?"

"This was sort of a work in progress when Mom bought it. The original owners had it on the market for a while but it didn't sell. They decided to do some upgrades to help that along and just as they finished both kitchens, they got a contract on the property. The prospective buyers asked them to hold off on any additional changes. They agreed, and two months later, the financing fell through. Mom was able to snap it up for a song. A total God thing."

Dave smiled. "I thought you hated it here."

Lisa lifted a shoulder. "Just because it isn't good for me doesn't make it bad for Mom. It's the first home she's ever owned, and I've never seen her so happy. The community has just smothered her in kindness, and Praise Tabernacle..." Her gaze turned distant. "It feels a lot like home to both of us."

Her words warmed Dave. He'd hoped she was a believer. "I knew there was something I liked about you. Church kid, huh?"

"Born and bred."

Dave leaned on the bar. Even after a day of hard labor, there was a slight scent of honeysuckles that clung to her hair, or maybe it was her clothes. It played havoc with his concentration, and he struggled to remember where the conversation had been headed. *Oh yeah, Praise Tabernacle.* "You like baseball?"

She waffled her hand back and forth. "I can take it or leave it. Why?"

"Because my kids and Jemma's kids have a game scheduled tomorrow afternoon after church. If you don't have anything to do, you could come out to the park and watch. Cheering for the Abundant Life Warriors is optional."

She snorted. "If I come, I'll be pulling for the Praise Tabernacle team."

"Good enough." Dave took a final drink, and the ice rattled in his glass when he set it down.

"You want a refill?" Lisa asked.

"No. I need to get home and put the finishing touches on tomorrow's sermon for the youth group."

And in that instant, just like last week, Lisa's expression

closed as if she'd slammed the shutters. "Oh...right...well." She stood and led the way to the front door. "You better get going then."

The change in her mood was so abrupt, Dave had no choice but to follow her to the door. He stepped onto the porch and managed to snag her hand. "I had a good time."

Lisa tugged her hand free and crossed her arms. "Thanks for the help. I'll see you...around." She took a step away from him and closed the door.

Dave stood there for several seconds. *What just happened?* He replayed the last few seconds of their conversation, looking for something to account for her sudden frostiness. He came up empty.

He walked to his truck, climbed inside, rested his head on the steering wheel, and did what he always did when life confused him. *Father, I don't get it. We were getting along so well. I even... well, for a while there, the OCD backed off. Can You help me figure this out? I like this girl.* He remembered the scene in the kitchen and owned up to reality. *I might like her too much for my own good, considering I just met her a week ago.* He took a couple of deep breaths. *You know I only want Your will for my life. I've accepted that that means the ministry, and I know You have the perfect helper for me.* Dave stared back at the house as the lights in the living room blinked off. *The perfect wife.*

Wife?

The word startled him out of the prayer. *Get real, Sisko.* He started the car. He had things to do, and part of that meant arranging a meeting with Jemma Hudson. Maybe she could give him some insight into Lisa.

———

LISA STOOD in the living room, her head resting against the door long after Dave pulled away from her house. *I need to get home and put the finishing touches on tomorrow's sermon.* The words had hit her like a bucket of ice water in the face. "Thanks for the reminder, Father."

She walked back to her bedroom, all enthusiasm for the evening's work gone. Dave was a good-looking, funny guy. She thought about the way he'd picked up the living room and his insistence on cleaning up before he'd called it a night. She added adorably quirky to the list of his good qualities. He was available, and most importantly, he was a Christian.

She was a healthy, single, Christian young woman who wanted a Christian man in her life more than just about anything. Lisa sat on her bed, flopped back on the mattress, and covered her eyes with her arms. Unfortunately, Dave was also the one thing he couldn't be, the one thing she refused to make room for in her life. Dave Sisko was a preacher, and she would never, ever, be a part of that lifestyle again.

SIX

Lisa looked up when Jemma fell into step beside her on the way out the door of Praise Tabernacle Sunday morning. "Hey," she said.

"Hey back." Jemma grabbed Lisa's arm and turned her toward a corner of the lobby, where they would be out of the way of the flow of people exiting the Sunday morning service. "Do you have plans for this afternoon?"

"Not really. Mom's going with her Sunday school class for their monthly lunch out. I was planning to go home and finish cleaning up from last night. Why?"

"I really need your help. Some of the kids are playing ball this afternoon—"

"I know. Dave told me about it before he left last night."

Jemma stepped back and studied her friend. "Dave was at your house last night, and the two of you made such a mess that you need to spend the day cleaning?" She fanned her face. "I need every detail."

"You know you're pathetic?"

"Completely. Start at the beginning."

Lisa rolled her eyes. "He came over to help me finish painting the bedrooms. After we were done and before I kicked him out in favor of a hot bubble bath and a good book, I fixed him a glass of tea. While consuming the afore mentioned beverage he invited me to the game, which I have decided to decline. There you have it. The whole tawdry story."

"Decline why?"

Lisa crossed her arms and turned slightly. Should she tell Jemma she liked the guy too much to spend any more time with him than necessary? *Not going there.* "I have stuff to do. Besides, I left Snowflake by herself all day yesterday. Repeating that today would only justify the objections Dave made when I brought her home."

Jemma's eyebrows climbed into her bangs. "I think thou doth protest too much."

"What?"

"Nothing," Jemma said. "Look, Heather was supposed to help me this afternoon. She just called to tell me she wasn't feeling well. I need an extra grown-up at the park. You won't have to do much. Keep score and organize snacks and drinks between innings. I'm coaching the team so I can't do those things."

"I—"

"Please?" Jemma added some best-friend whining to her voice. "I promise I won't let the big bad enemy youth pastor bother you."

"Cute."

"I'll see you at the park at two." Jemma turned and headed out the door.

"I didn't—"

"You're a sweetheart. I'll see you in a bit."

Lisa watched her go. Speechless...railroaded...and spending her afternoon at the ballpark.

DAVE LEANED against the backstop fence and watched his kids practice. He'd arrived a bit early. He didn't know if Lisa would take him up on his invitation, but he wanted to have time for a few words with Jemma before the chance was lost under the friendly rivalry of the game.

Jemma had been a big help to him as he'd settled into his first youth pastor position. A couple of years older, with a few years shepherding the youth at Praise Tabernacle under her belt, she'd almost become the big sister he'd never had. Jemma wouldn't break a confidence, even if he asked, but if there was anything she could share about what made the lovely Lisa tick, he'd have it before the day was done.

The crack of the bat on the ball jerked his attention to the batter's box just in time to see Willie Jenkins toss the bat aside and sprint for first base. Dave's eyes searched the sky and found the ball sailing high and long over the head of the left fielder. He clapped and whistled. "Way to go, Willie!"

He stood there while Willie rounded the bases and then stepped behind the plate to give the boy a high five as he brought it all the way home. "That's what I'm talking about," Dave said.

Willie, tall and built like a brick wall, clasped his arms around Dave in a bear hug and lifted him off the ground.

When Dave's feet were planted on terra firma once more, he pounded Willie's back. "I hope you saved one of those for later."

The young man grinned. "Just call me your secret weapon."

Dave returned the smile, amused at the boundless self-confidence of youth.

Gravel crunched in the parking area as the van and a couple of cars from Praise Tabernacle arrived. Dave gave Willie a final pat on the shoulder and loped across the grassy apron surrounding the field. He arrived in time to see Jemma swing a heavy bag of equipment over her shoulder. Dave took it from her and leaned in to kiss her cheek.

"You guys got here early," Jemma said, yanking the bill of his cap over his eyes and laughing when he stumbled.

"Hey." Dave straightened his cap and took a couple of quick steps to catch back up to her. "Just warming up."

"Should we worry?"

"I'd concede defeat now if I were you."

Jemma laughed. "I just bet." She clapped her hands and motioned for her kids to circle around. "Our opponent says we're already beaten. What say you?"

A couple of dozen voices lifted. "No way!"

"I didn't think so." She waved at the field. "Go get warmed up. Game starts in twenty minutes."

The kids dispersed, but Dave lingered at Jemma's side. "Can we talk?"

"Sure." She must have seen something serious in his expression because she frowned. "What's up?"

Dave looked at his feet. He had her attention but didn't know where to start. He scuffed at the dirt with a worn athletic shoe. "It's not a what, but a who."

Jemma narrowed her eyes and barely concealed her smirk. "Lisa."

"How did you—?"

"She's mentioned you a time or two."

Her comment made Dave's pulse race, and he straightened as if the increased pounding of his heart were pumping life into his spine like air into an inner tube. "She talks about me?" He waited for Jemma's answer with the anticipation of a kid on Christmas Eve.

Jemma grinned at him. "Down boy." She studied him. "You got a thing for my new bestie?"

"No..."

Her eyebrows rose.

"Maybe?"

Jemma crossed her arms and waited.

"I mean, yes. I like her. I think I could more than like her." Dave paced four steps away, turned, and ran his hands through his hair. "What's not to like? She's beautiful, she's a believer, we get along fine...most of the time."

"Most of the time? What's going on the rest of the time?"

"That's what I wanted to talk to you about. I've only known

her for a week, but I feel a connection I can't ignore. I'd like the chance to explore that, but every time we talk, she ends up with this shuttered look on her face, and it's like she can't get away from me fast enough. So, if you can do it without breaking a confidence, I hoped you could tell me what I'm missing."

Jemma chewed her bottom lip and stared across the field. "There are some things we've talked about that I'm not comfortable repeating. I can give you a nudge in the right direction though. Think about your conversations. What was the last thing you said before the shutters came down?"

"I've done that. I can't think of a thing I've said that was out of line."

Jemma brought her gaze back to his, the look on her face almost maternal. "I didn't say anything about you being out of line. Look, she's got some baggage from her childhood."

"Don't we all?"

"Exactly." Jemma patted his arm. "Pray about it, and just be yourself. The next time she shuts you down stop right there and consider what you just said. Then make her talk to you. You are uniquely qualified to address her particular hang-ups."

"But you're not going to tell me why."

Jemma twisted an imaginary key between her lips and tossed it away. "No can do."

Fresh tires churned the gravel as a new car turned into the parking lot. Lisa waved from behind the wheel, and they both returned the gesture. Dave took a step forward, and Jemma stopped him with a hand on his arm. "But I will say that I've got a very good feeling about this."

LISA WATCHED the game from the bleachers with a few dozen parents, siblings, and miscellaneous members of both youth groups who'd decided to take advantage of the mild spring weather. The competition was intense but friendly with the lead bouncing back and forth between Praise Tabernacle and Abundant Life.

But more than the game, Lisa found herself watching Dave. He loved his kids. It was apparent in every interaction, from the way he encouraged the player who struck out for the fourth time to the way he dealt with the loud-mouthed young man who'd spewed an ugly insult when that final swing failed to connect. While the game continued, Dave took each boy involved in the conflict aside for a quiet conversation. Then the three of them met together, and Lisa saw smiles, handshakes, and bowed heads. Dave loved, and he was loved in return. The knowledge warmed a chilly spot in Lisa's heart.

It was the bottom of the ninth inning, and the score was tied at five runs each. The next run would decide the game, and it was Abundant Life's turn at bat. Lisa made a note on her score sheet and looked up when she heard a collective groan from the field. She bit her lip and felt her chest tighten with the certainty that the game was about to be over. The tall redheaded kid stepping to the plate had already sent two balls over the fence. He took his place, gave his bat a couple of practice swings, and pointed it toward left field.

The kids from Abundant Life began to chant, "Go Willie...go Willie...go Willie..."

Lisa put her head in her hands, closed her eyes, and waited for the end. The crack of ball meeting the bat, the groans of the defeated, and the cheers of the victors. Five minutes later, she stood next to an open ice chest handing out ice cream bars in a cloud of dry-ice vapor.

"You got an extra one of those?"

She looked up to find Dave beside her. "To the victor go the spoils?"

Dave grinned. "Only if all the kids have had one."

"The kids could all have two and there would still be plenty. Jemma must have emptied the freezer-section of the Harrison

Market. What's your pleasure? I have Fudgsicles, Eskimo pies, or ice cream sandwiches."

"Which is your favorite?" he asked.

"Hmm..." She pretended to give it some thought. "Ice cream sandwiches."

"I'll take two of those." Dave accepted the treat, smiling when their hands brushed. He pointed at the empty bleachers. "Join me?"

Lisa looked around. There were no more kids in line. "Looks like you're my last customer." She closed the ice chest and followed Dave to the top row of seats. She settled beside him and accepted the frozen treat. From their vantage point they watched as kids from both groups broke into friendly clusters, eating their treats, and holding conversations that failed to reach the summit of the stands.

"I'm glad you came," Dave said.

"Well, Jemma didn't give me a whole lot of choice, but I'm glad I did too."

Dave took a bite and leaned against the back rest as he chewed. "Everything dry out all right at home?"

Lisa nodded. "The rooms look amazing. Thanks again for your help."

"I enjoyed it." He turned his head and met her gaze. "Know what else I'd really enjoy?"

Looking into Dave's eyes was like looking into the waters of the Caribbean. Blue and calming and deeper than it first appeared. Her mind screamed words of warning, but her heart wanted to know what lay under the surface. She swallowed. "No...what?"

His smile was lazy, his voice a whisper, his gaze intent. "Dinner with a pretty girl. This Friday night. Maybe around six?"

He hadn't touched her, but Lisa felt like every synapse in her body might short circuit. "I..." *Don't do it.* The internal battle raged, a tug of war between her head and her heart, childhood hurts against adult possibilities. *Father, I can't do this to either of us.*

"Hey." The voice came from field below, one of Dave's kids,

the beefy red head, standing next to the ice chest. "Can I have another?"

Lisa stood, grateful for the interruption. "Coming."

Dave grabbed her hand and pulled her back to her place next to him. "Help yourself. We're in a meeting."

The snort was audible. "Yeah, right."

"Just get your ice cream and take a hike. The pretty lady and I have business."

The kid made kissy sounds, but did as he was told.

Lisa's heart took a nose dive when Dave's ears turned hot pink. *Look at him, Father. He's so sweet. I don't know what to do.*

Dave cleared his throat. "So, dinner?"

Lisa looked away, searching for the best way to say no.

Do you trust me, Daughter?

"Yes." Lisa wasn't sure whose question she answered but Dave smiled and the heaviness in her chest lightened.

"Outstanding." He stood up and held out his hand. "Let me help you down."

"What's your hurry? I'm not done with my ice cream."

"Well hurry up, woman. I need to get busy. The sooner I get the next five days out of the way, the better."

Enchanted by his words, Lisa allowed him to pull her to her feet. Dave kept her hand in his, and when they reached the bottom of the bleachers, he brushed her knuckles with a kiss. She smiled up into his eyes, and couldn't remember how she'd reached the ground. Had she walked or floated?

SEVEN

THE LATE MORNING sunlight pierced Lisa's eyes Friday like a javelin thrown by a gold medal Olympian. She snapped her lids closed, groaned, and turned in her bed. The movement made her freshly aware of the pain in her joints that she'd fought to ignore all day yesterday. The denial she'd clung to over the previous twenty-four hours evaporated, and truth took up residence in both sides of the Garcia duplex. Lisa had the flu, no doubt the same strain she'd spent the last three days nursing her mother through. Mom was on the mend, but Lisa felt like...

"No...no...no," she whispered, her voice a harsh croak in the empty room. "I've got a date tonight." Lisa pulled the comforter over her head. *I had a date tonight.* The afterthought settled and weighed down her already heavy heart. She'd have to call Dave and cancel.

Lisa flopped onto her back. She didn't have to call him right this minute. She might feel better as the day wore on. In an effort to prove to herself that she wasn't as sick as she felt, Lisa pushed herself up and sat on the side of the bed. When she opened her eyes, she felt the heat of a fever burning behind them. The room swam. Lisa gave in to the vertigo and collapsed back into the pillows. A chill seized her, and she burrowed under the covers. *Who am I kidding?*

Her hand snaked out from under the comforter, and she fumbled for the phone on the nightstand. Lisa found it, and her hand froze. She still didn't have his number. Her body slumped deeper into the pillows. How...? *Jemma would have it.* She pulled the phone under the covers and punched in numbers with a trembling finger.

"Hey, Lisa."

"I need a favor." The words croaked out of her hoarse throat, and Lisa cringed at the raspy sound.

"You sound awful. What's wrong?"

"Flu, I think." She moved the phone away from her face as a fit of coughing overcame her. Once she caught her breath, she returned to her explanation. "I've been nursing Mom through it all week."

"The family who cares, shares," Jemma quipped.

"Yeah."

"What's the favor?"

"I need Dave's phone number. We had a date tonight—"

"Oh..."

"I need to let him know."

Jemma rattled off the number.

Lisa looked around for something to write with and on. "Hang on. I don't have a pen."

"Stay where you're at. I'll text it to you. Do you need anything else?"

"Pra—" A second fit of coughing choked off the word. "Prayer," she gasped.

"You've got that. Call Dave and go back to sleep. I'll be there with chicken soup and Tylenol by the time you wake up."

"Thanks. Wait...what?"

"I'm coming to take care of you and your mom."

"No, you aren't."

"Yes, I am. You need to eat and you need meds. If I know you, and I do, you haven't been shopping this week, and if you have medicine, you can't find the bottle."

Lisa closed her eyes and tried to remember where she'd last seen the bottle of pain relievers. Her mind's eye conjured a clear picture of an empty bottle on her mother's nightstand. *I need a keeper.* She shook her head. "This is ugly stuff, Jemma."

"I nursed Heather through it last week, so I've already been exposed. And think about this. What will your mom do if she knows you're next door, sick and by yourself?"

Lisa groaned at the thought of her mother suffering through a second round of this nasty bug because she'd spent the day nursing her.

"Suck it up, girlfriend, it's what friends do. Save your energy for getting better, and stop arguing. Dave's number is coming your way."

The phone went dead in her hand and immediately buzzed with an incoming text. Her conversation with Dave was brief as she explained about her need to cancel their plans.

"Do you need anything," he asked, unconsciously repeating Jemma's earlier question.

"Not really. Jemma is on her way over. I tried to talk her out of it, but she's convinced I need a nursemaid."

"It's what friends...and ministers do."

"Yeah, well..."

"Tell you what," he continued. "Why don't I call you after we're finished at the house tomorrow? I know you don't feel like going out, but if you're up to some company by then, I can bring dinner, and we could watch a movie or something."

"I don't know."

"An early night, I promise. I have to put the finishing touches on Sunday morning's message. Pretty please," he wheedled.

Lisa's eyes burned, and talking without coughing was a struggle. She gave in with a single word. "Sure."

Saturday afternoon Dave returned to his house with more than a little satisfaction. The day couldn't have gone better. His little crew had made great strides. The outside of Mrs. Craig's little two-story house wore a shiny new coat of white paint. It looked wonderful with the black shutters. The new fence complimented everything with a heavy layer of weather proofing over the bare wood. Next week he'd put most of the group on the yard work while the rest painted the interior walls. The project would finish on time.

Chester danced around his feet while he carried tools from the truck to the shop. He needed to get cleaned up and give Lisa a call. He'd missed seeing her today and hoped she was feeling up to a little company. She'd enjoy hearing about their progress.

When his phone rang, he dropped the hammers on the workbench and grabbed it from the pouch at his waist.

"Hello."

"Dave, its Brian. You need to get over to Harry's house right now." Brian, a junior from Abundant Life's youth group sounded frantic, his words stumbling over each other.

"Brian, take a breath and slow down. What's up with Harry? I thought he was spending the weekend at your house."

"He is...I mean, he did last night, but he went home for a while this afternoon while I was at work. I called to let him know I was on my way home. And man...Tricia just dumped him. He's talking nonsense, and I'm worried. I'm on my way over there."

"Me too. Call his folks."

"They're headed home, but they're a good four hours away."

Dave slammed the door to the shop, dodged around the dog, and jumped into his truck. Teenagers changed their minds about who they *loved* like some people changed their socks. It came with the territory, but Tricia's timing couldn't be worse.

Gravel spun under Dave's tires as he threw the truck into gear and raced out of the drive. Harry's parents were on a rare trip out of town to welcome a new grandchild. Harry was eighteen and could certainly take care of himself for a few days under normal circumstances, but... *Does Tricia know about the depression and the suicide attempt two years ago?* Dave shook the question aside. It didn't matter. All that mattered was that he get to Harry's house before the kid did something stupid.

LISA PACED the living room Saturday evening, growing angrier each time her restless steps took her past the clock. *I should have known better.* She chewed her bottom lip and let the silent rebuke sink in as she came in view of the time once again. Eight PM. No phone call, no text, no note tied to the leg of a pigeon. Nothing.

She'd felt much better today, and, despite her misgivings about spreading whatever bug this was to someone else, she'd looked forward to spending some time with Dave. But he wasn't here and obviously couldn't be bothered to call and let her know why.

Snowflake twisted around her feet. Lisa scooped her up, cuddled her to her chest, and couldn't stop the smile when the little engine started to purr against her heart.

She jumped when the phone rang. The tinkling ringtone told her it was her mother.

"Hey, Mom."

"How's my baby girl?"

"Better. You?"

"Just tired," she answered. "I know it's early but I was headed to bed and wanted to check on you first."

Lisa grinned at her mother's thinly veiled curiosity and accepted it as a byproduct of living next door to each other. She'd mentioned, in an earlier conversation, that Dave planned to stop by sometime this evening. It wasn't hard to picture her mother keeping watch out her front window, hoping to catch of glimpse of the new guy in her daughter's life.

Yeah, right.

"I'm thinking about bed too."

"Really? But I thought...I mean...your young man—"

"I guess something came up." The words tasted bitter on Lisa's tongue. Her mother had spent her life making excuses for a negligent man. Lisa didn't intend to relive that mistake. "Get some rest, Mom. I'll call you in the morning." She disconnected the call and looked out the window. The hopeful part of her longed to see Dave's headlights in her drive. The realistic part of her buried hope under a lifetime of disappointment.

Her stomach growled. She put Snowflake back on the floor, stomped into her kitchen, and yanked the pantry door open. She surveyed her options, sadly reminded that she needed to buy groceries. A box of crackers caught her eye, and she yanked them off the shelf. There was a block of cheddar cheese in the fridge, and Lisa convinced herself that cheese, crackers, and her last can of soda were just what she'd been craving all day.

She sat at one side of the table with her dinner and pulled an envelope free from the stack of mail on the other side. While she nibbled, she made a list of things she needed from the store. If she didn't die overnight, she'd go shopping right after church tomorrow.

Die?

Well, that was a huge exaggeration, but what if it wasn't? Lisa slammed the pen down on the table and shoved her chair back. Would Dave know? Would he care? Or did that higher calling that he'd given his life to insulate him from human emotion?

Her hands clenched into fists. Late dinners, missed school events, broken promises, vacations with just Mom. She blinked. *When did I go from Dave to Dad?* Lisa sucked in a deep breath, forced her hands to relax, and shoved aside the unproductive anger that thoughts of her father often bred. She cleaned up her snack and took one last look out the window before she switched off the lights.

Lisa's whole life had been spent waiting for the most important man in her life to notice her existence. If David Elijah Sisko thought he could be the next man to put her into that position...he could think again.

EIGHT

For Lisa, the next six days could be measured in ignored phone calls and text messages. Dave had tried to contact her at least a dozen times a day, and a dozen times a day, Lisa ignored him.

There were times she was tempted to answer. Dave was cute in a shy, gentle way. If she admitted the truth—and since the conversation was being held somewhere between her own heart and mind, she gave herself the luxury of honesty—she liked him. But liking him made him dangerous. So, despite the little voice between her ears that told her she was being childish, she ignored the calls and let his persistence frustrate her. Every time she saw his name on the small screen, she took a second to remember her lonely Saturday night. And she allowed that memory to strengthen her resolve. Never again would she take second place in a man's life.

Ignoring him served a second purpose as well. Lisa had given her word when she'd signed up for the Christmas-in-April project. Her conscience wouldn't allow her to skip the last day of work. That meant seeing Dave. She hoped that by the time they were face to face on Saturday, he'd be as irritated with her as she was with him. All she wanted was for him to assign her a job and get out of her way. Once the day was done, there'd be no reason to ever see him again.

Lisa left her house Saturday morning and paused on her porch to take a deep breath. Well, at least she tried. The air she pulled into her lungs was thick and sticky with humidity. The seventy-eight-degree temperature felt more like ninety as sweat popped from her pores and plastered her cotton shirt to her skin.

"Yuck." She plucked at the damp fabric. Spring had been one of her favorite times in California. If this was a hint of what a Texas spring was like, she'd never survive the next few weeks. She didn't want to think about what summer might bring.

She joined the line of cars parked in front of Mrs. Craig's house and sat for a minute admiring the work she'd help accomplish. With the peeling paint replaced and the fence rebuilt, the sturdy little two-story barely resembled the neglected structure they'd started with. Even the old oak tree that grew next to the house looked refreshed with its spreading branches decked out in newly budded leaves.

Lisa saw the other volunteers gathering at the porch. She'd timed her arrival perfectly. In time to get an assignment, but no time for any personal conversation. When she opened the car door, the heat hit her like a physical punch. Between trying to stay cool and dodging Dave, it promised to be a long day.

ENTHUSIASM for the project had waned a bit now that they'd hit the four-week mark. Dave accepted that as normal, grateful they'd completed the hardest jobs early in the process. Today there were only eight volunteers, and Dave had no trouble spotting Lisa when she slipped in from the side of the yard. She kept her head down, and he didn't need anyone to tell him that her nearly late arrival had been orchestrated perfectly. Lisa needn't worry. He'd spent the whole week trying to apologize for and explain about last week.

She obviously didn't want to hear it. With the exception of necessary instructions, he had no intention of invading her space today, or ever.

He portioned out the remaining tasks, keeping the four younger members of his team outside to work on the yard and sending the rest inside to paint the interior walls. He looked at the sky and saw the beginnings of dark clouds on the horizon. The heat and humidity told him a storm was brewing. His gaze went to the old storm shelter in the back corner of the yard. A prickle of apprehension ran up his spine. He shook his head, amused at is sense of foreboding. They'd be long gone before the storm, if there was one, arrived.

LISA TROOPED UP THE STAIRS. The second floor consisted of two small bedrooms divided by a tiny bath. The volunteers were spread pretty thin today, and she'd offered to do these rooms while the other three took on the much larger rooms on the ground floor. The existing paint was a hideous shade of sherbet orange in one room and lime green in the other. As much as she despised plain white walls, in this case the change would be a blessing. Lisa cocked her head. It would likely take two coats of the white to cover the bright colors. *Let's see what we've got.* She stepped to a blank wall, dipped a brush in the paint, and wrote I MISS THE BEACH in big white letters. She studied the result, satisfied with the coverage and resigned to an all-day job. Lisa put her earbuds in, cranked up her music, and got started. Sweat trickled down the side of her head, and she swiped it away. Nothing she couldn't handle as long as she didn't suffocate in the still, hot air.

First things first. She took a gallon of the paint and poured some into a small plastic bucket. With a medium brush, she began the tedious job of painting around the windows and doors. This was the part that would take the most time. At least someone had taped them off earlier. Lisa was grateful for their help. Once she had this part done, she could use a roller on the walls, and things would move along much more quickly.

With half a room completed and the music blasting, the tap on her shoulder took her by surprise. Lisa jerked around, the roller in her hand slinging paint in a wide arc, smirking when Dave jumped back to avoid the spatter. She swiped the earbuds free, and glared at Dave. "What?"

Dave pointed at the wall and the white letters of Lisa's earlier test. "This is a wall, not a message board." He looked at the paint on the floor and shook his head.

Lisa narrowed her eyes. He was obviously loaded for bear, and she could accommodate him. Last time she checked, she'd been the one stood up. She laid the roller in the pan, retrieved her brush, and crossed the room to an unpainted wall. GET LOST!!!!

Dave sucked in air. "We have to finish this project today. There isn't time for you to play in the paint."

Lisa faced Dave with her hands on her hips. "I'm well aware of our time constraints. I wasn't playing, I was testing the coverage." She pointed to her second message. "Now do us both a favor and take your OCD back down the stairs. I have work to do. Solitary work." She replaced the earbuds and glared as she raised the volume before turning her back and attacking the wall with a vengeance that would have done the *Home Makeover* crew proud.

DAVE RETREATED, stung by her words and his conscience. Lisa was doing a great job. What did he care if she played tic-tac-toe on the walls as long as they got painted? He'd gone up there to see if she needed help. The beach thing had irritated him. Probably because it seemed like another reminder that she wanted nothing further to do with him. He brought his hand down on the stair rail. All he'd wanted all week was a chance to explain and apologize.

Aggravating, confounded, stubborn woman. His feet hit the bottom riser when a wail rose from outside.

Tornado sirens.

"Lisa, get down here!" Dave yelled up the steps before turning to herd his other charges out the door. He shooed the three outside and hurried to the kitchen in time to see Mrs. Craig pulling another batch of her cookies out of the oven. He met her halfway across the room and took her arm.

"We need to go."

The older woman nodded and turned off the gas. "Don't worry, Dave. This old place has weathered more than its fair share of Texas storms."

He didn't answer, just took a firmer grip on her arm and guided her through the back door. Outside, he was relieved to see the group working in the yard already had the cellar open and waiting. He handed Mrs. Craig off to one of the volunteers and glanced at the sky. No rain yet, but the wind was swirling the leaves, and the clouds were heavy and ominous. He motioned to the cellar. "Everybody in."

They hurried to the cement vault and trooped down steep stairs. Dave blinked in the gloom and fumbled for his phone. He opened the flashlight app and swung it around, counting faces. He was one short. His heart plunged to his feet. Where was Lisa? He climbed four of the steps and looked at the house as the first drops of rain pelted him. He closed his eyes against the sting. His memory conjured the image of Lisa turning up her music. *She hadn't heard him or the siren.*

Dave looked back down the steps. "Stay put and close the door. Lisa's still painting." He raced across the yard, gaining the door as hail began to fall. The increasing wind yanked the door out of his hand. It slammed against the house with a crash. He raced up the stairs and found Lisa starting another wall. "Lisa!"

She turned, frowned at him, and yanked out the earbuds. "I told you to get lost."

Aggravating, confounded, stubborn woman. Dave didn't waste the breath to say the words aloud or offer an explanation. He crossed the room, grabbed Lisa, and tossed her over his shoulder. The house groaned and creaked as he took the stairs two at a time, with Lisa kicking against his hold the whole time. He yanked the door open. Outside, the howl of the wind competed with the siren, and the sky pelted quarter-sized hail. Instead of trying to make the cellar, he turned toward the closet under the stairs. It was small and in the center of the house. It would have to do.

Dave threw open the door, pulled the cord on the light, and slid Lisa to her feet.

She shoved him away. "What are you doing?"

Dave ignored her and searched the small space for anything that might help protect them if the situation grew worse. He saw two bicycle helmets on an upper shelf. He grabbed them and plopped one on Lisa's head before donning the second. "Fasten that."

"You're just full of yourself today, aren't you?"

Dave took a step closer. "I know you're mad at me, but this isn't the time—"

"You don't have a clue." She leaned into his space and glared.

"I'd have a clue if you'd talk to me. You might have a clue if you'd listen."

"I've had enough lies from your kind to last me a lifetime. Now let me out of here." She yelped as something crashed outside.

The light went out.

Dave felt her grab onto his shirt. "What's going on?"

He pulled her close. "Tornado warning."

"Tornado?"

"Can't you hear the sirens?"

She cocked her head for a second, and her eyes went round. He heard her swallow. "We don't have those in L.A. Earthquakes are our natural disaster of choice."

"Don't worry, it's usually nothing." The house shuddered around them. "But sometimes it's not nothing." He pushed her to her knees on the floor and crouched over her. "Jesus, be our protection in the storm. Shelter us, shelter those in the cellar."

Lisa added her prayer to his. "Father, we need You."

Glass broke, and it felt as if the air had been sucked out of the closet. Something big and heavy slammed into the house with enough force to shake the foundation. Lisa screamed and Dave tightened his grip. "I've got you."

NINE

THE NOISE STOPPED AS SUDDENLY as it started, leaving an eerie silence that seemed louder than the storm in the darkness of the closet. Dave almost preferred the howling of the wind. He unfolded himself and eased away from Lisa. He felt her jerk when the light from his phone filled the small space.

He extended a hand. "Are you OK?"

Lisa took the hand. "I think so." She straightened. "Is it over?"

"Probably." He tilted his head and couldn't stop the grin.

"What?"

"Nothing." He tapped the helmet he'd shoved onto her head. "You're pretty adorable as a purple unicorn."

Lisa yanked it off and examined it with her own light. "Cute." She swung the tiny beam in his direction. "And you really are my hero, Peter."

"Peter?"

"Take a look."

He tugged the helmet free and brought it into the light. Spiderman flew across the dome of yellow plastic, spraying his web. "Glad I could help." He tossed the helmet onto the shelf and reached for the door. "Let's get out of here and check on the others." He twisted the knob and gave a push.

Nothing.

He put his hands on his hips. "The wind must have twisted the frame or something. It's stuck."

"Well, come on Spiderman. Put some muscle behind it."

Dave took a step back, lunged, and shoved his shoulder into the door. It didn't give a centimeter. Dave rubbed his shoulder and prepared to try again. After the second shove produced no more result than the first, Lisa added her weight to the third. Nothing moved.

"Sorry," he said. "but I don't think we're going anywhere for a while."

"We have to get out of here. Mom was home. What if...?" Lisa let the words hang and yanked her phone out of her pocket. She keyed in numbers and frowned before slapping the instrument with her free hand. "Come on!"

Dave looked at his own screen. The words *no service* mocked him from the upper left corner. "Storm must have damaged the cell tower."

She looked around the small space, her eyes darting from corner to corner.

He clasped his hands over hers. "Look at me." Dave hoped his smile was confident when she met his gaze. "Now, take a deep breath." Her brown eyes remained locked on his as she did what he asked.

"Better?"

She gave a single jerk of her head in response.

"I know you're worried about your mom, and not being able to check on her is scary, but panic won't get us out of here. We need to be patient. People know where we are." Well, he conceded to himself, that might be a little bit of a lie. The guys he'd left in the cellar knew he'd come back in the house for Lisa. If they were OK, they'd be looking. He swallowed back the bitter taste of his own anxiety and squeezed her fingers. "We have great emergency management teams. They'll have us out of here in no time." He let go of her hands. "But you might want to save your battery, just in case."

Lisa sighed, slid to the floor, and waited for Dave to do the same before she killed the light. They sat in silence for a moment or two, the darkness thick and still except for their breathing.

Dave drummed his fingers on his leg. Maybe he could get her to listen now. He bowed his head to his knees. *Father, if You've given us this chance to talk, I don't want to waste it. Please give me the right words.*

"I'm sorry about last week," he said.

"Me, too," Lisa whispered.

A few more beats of silence. At least she hadn't shut him down. Her words from earlier reverberated in his mind until he couldn't keep the question in any longer. "What did you mean earlier when you said you'd had enough lies from *my kind* to last a lifetime?"

He heard Lisa sigh. "It's a really long story."

Dave gave the blocked door a solid rap with his knuckles. "What else have we got to do?"

Her voice was soft when it came out of the dark. "My dad was a preacher."

She paused for so long that Dave worried that might be the extent of her explanation. He heard a sniff and didn't know whether to reach for her or wait. He chose to wait.

"He was a master at building something from nothing," Lisa finally said. "He specialized in reviving churches where the membership had fallen. He'd go in, and it wouldn't be long before he had everyone left in the congregation committed to an outreach program. He'd organize committees, the committees would organize activities, the activities would bring the people, and the people would crowd the pews. In three or four years, the church would be involved in a thriving building program. Once the church had a nice new building filled with dedicated people, Dad would get bored, uproot Mom and me, and the cycle would start all over again. By the time I left for college, he was rallying his fifth or sixth congregation."

"He sounds like an amazing man of God."

"He was," Lisa agreed. "He had a real gift." Another pause, another sniff. "I grew up begging God to take it away from him."

"Why would you do that?"

Dave didn't think the noise he heard from Lisa was a laugh. "Because we always had a church, but we never had a family. I played softball all through high school. Dad never attended a single game. Dinner was just Mom and me five or six nights a week because something or someone needed him more than we did. He wasn't at my graduation, didn't help transport me to college. And vacations? Dad financed some great trips, but he was always too busy to travel with us. The Bible calls the pastor the shepherd of the flock. Dad took that role very seriously."

This time when she paused, Dave was sure he heard a giggle.

"I've often wondered when he found time to get Mom pregnant. He knew we needed him. There were constant promises to Mom and me to try harder, to pay more attention, to slow down. He just needed to do this one more thing..."

An outright sob filled the darkness.

"He worked himself into an early grave at the age of fifty. I figure he's in heaven now, organizing the Second Coming." Her voice was bitter.

Dave weighed her words and took the time to see Saturday from Lisa's point of view. More than a disappointment. Another broken promise by a busy minister. He recalled his questioning of Jemma days ago and her comment that he was *uniquely qualified* to address Lisa's hesitancy. He rubbed his hands down his face and looked to the dark ceiling. *Messed that up.*

Lisa wasn't finished. "Don't get me wrong. I admire ministers and what they do. I know how important they are to the church and the twenty-first-century work of God. But I don't want to be a part of it. I won't live that way. I won't raise a family that way."

She shifted, and her hand landed on Dave's knee. Dave laced his fingers with hers.

"I like you...too much," she said. "There's a silly, romantic part of me that makes me want to forget everything I lived through. Then there's the logical, realistic side that won't let me past it. I know you had a good reason for standing me up. There will always be a good reason."

Dave squeezed her fingers. No one understood the adult fears and insecurities bred by a deprived childhood more than he did. *Father, help me make her understand.* He raised her hand to his lips and brushed her knuckles with a kiss. She didn't pull away, and he counted that as a victory.

"Thanks for being honest with me." And even though she'd denied needing the facts of Saturday's emergency, he gave them to her anyway, leaving out the names she didn't need to know. "The young man had taken pills by the time we got there. We managed to get him to the hospital, and they were able to save his life. It was touch-and-go for several hours, and when his parents finally arrived, they needed me for support until the danger passed. Since we're being honest, let me say that calling you never crossed my mind until the next day. We know how that went."

Lisa struggled to pull her hand from his grasp. "You must think I'm a horrible person."

Dave held on tighter. "No, you're just wounded, like all of us. I'm not going to lie to you. I take what I do very seriously. As a minister, there are always going to be emergencies, people who need me at unexpected times, people whose demands on my time and attention might seem unreasonable to my family. But I think the way your father handled his calling was wrong."

"How so?"

"There's a verse in First Timothy that says that the man who doesn't provide for his family, the people of his own house, is worse than an unbeliever. That's sort of cobbled together, but I can show you the verse when we get out of here."

"We never lacked for physical things," Lisa said.

"No, but you did without his time and attention. You grew up questioning his love. Providing for a family is more than just money." Dave paused and let that soak in while he gathered his thoughts.

"Lisa, I can't make up for what your father didn't give you any more than you can make up for the family I longed for in that orphanage. The past is the past. At some point in our lives, we have to move beyond the things we did without and trust God for the things of the future."

Overcome with the need to see her face, he fumbled with his phone and, when the light came on, laid it on the shelf behind him. He'd heard her tears in the darkness, but the sight of them undid him. He cupped her face in his hands, used his thumbs to wipe away the moisture, and met her liquid gaze.

"We've only known each other for a month, and despite what I'm beginning to feel, I'm not going to pressure you." The noise of a chainsaw cut through the silence, and dust rained down on them as something above them shifted. Dave scrambled to his feet and pulled Lisa to hers. "We aren't going to be in here much longer. Will you promise me that you'll pray about what I've said?"

She bit her lip and nodded.

The roar of the chain saw died.

"You guys all right in there?" The words came from a muffled voice.

Their answer came in unison. "Yes!"

"Great. Back away from the door, we'll have you out of there in a jif."

Lisa pulled him as far into the back corner as possible. "Thanks for not giving up on me. Can I call you in a day or two, after I've had some time to sort some things out?"

"I'm counting on it." Dave had time for a single stolen kiss before the door gave a final shrieking protest and swung free of the mangled frame.

TEN

LISA SETTLED herself and her coffee into the porch swing just before sunrise on Sunday morning. She sipped the steaming liquid as the sun rose in the eastern sky, painting the feathery clouds with fiery reds and oranges. From where Lisa sat, spring was alive with birdsong and vibrant shades of newly sprouted green. It all seemed incredibly peaceful.

She knew better.

Across town...across the bridge...havoc reigned.

Yesterday's tornado had crossed Harrison in a zigzag path, touching down at odd intervals like a toddler on a sugar high racing from one toy to another. But this was no youngster in need of a nap. This was destruction on a scale Lisa had never experienced. On its way through town, the fickle wind had laid waste to a dozen houses in Harrison before it uprooted the enormous tree outside of Mrs. Craig's dining room. Disappointed with its new plaything, it dropped on the tree on the house before it skittered away.

Lisa shuddered at the memory of the crash, thankful for Dave's quick thinking in getting them into the closet. The tree had blocked the door and held them captive, but another twelve inches to the west, and that closet would have been toothpicks, and them with it. They'd come out of their hiding space grateful to be alive only to learn the dreadful truth. Mrs. Craig's house, along with a handful of others, was lost. Minimal damage given the circumstances. But Yellow Veil had not been so lucky.

The damage across the bridge was devastating. Ruined businesses, destroyed homes, foundations wiped completely clean of the buildings they once supported. This had been the fate of Abundant Life Church. The building was simply gone.

Lisa's hands shook so badly she set her cup aside. Her heart ached for everyone affected, but especially for Dave. She closed her eyes. *Father, please just be there for them today.* Once the sun was up she'd go offer what physical help she could, but—

"I thought I heard someone out here."

Mom stepped onto the porch with her own cup. The sight of her mom safe and sound brought tears to Lisa's eyes. She'd been so worried yesterday, but God had her back, just like always.

Lisa made room on the swing. "Morning."

Mom joined her, swiping Lisa's cheek with a kiss as she settled. "Morning, baby. Mercy, would you look at the colors out here. How can everything look so lush and peaceful when the world is shambles just a few miles away?"

"I know. I still can't believe it. I'm so glad you're OK."

Mom shook her head. "Me? I wasn't anywhere close to the storm. I'm the one who's glad today. If it hadn't been for the quick thinking of that young man of yours, I might have lost you."

Her mother's comment twisted the lid off the can of worms Lisa had been trying to contain since the day before. Surely it was wrong, even selfish, to think about Dave and his romantic suggestions at a time like this. There were much more urgent concerns right now, weren't there?

"Talk to me, baby girl."

Lisa gave her a glance. "What?"

Mom smiled. "You had your nose wrinkled in that I've-got-a-problem face you've been making since you couldn't sound out your library words in first grade. It's a dead giveaway that something's bothering you."

Lisa raised a hand and indicated the world beyond the porch. "Where do I start?"

"Um hum." Mom sifted so that they faced each other. "As horrible as this twist of nature is, no one died, and things can be replaced. And don't you dare frown at me young lady. I'm not marginalizing anyone's loss. I'll be lining up to help where I can, same as you." She studied Lisa with knowing eyes. "Your nose wrinkling wouldn't have anything to do with a certain young pastor over in the next town, would it?"

Lisa looked away from her mom and reached out to retrieve her cup before giving the swing a gentle push. "It's impossible, Mom."

"How so?"

"How so?" The words were sharp as she lunged to her feet, setting the swing to rocking so violently, her mom was forced to hold her sloshing cup away from her lap. "Sorry." Lisa slung the lukewarm contents of her cup onto the lawn, set her mug on the porch, and paced away a few steps before turning to face her mother.

"How can you even ask me that after the way Daddy treated me...you"—she raised her hands—"us?" She hugged the support and leaned her head against it, her words a desolate whisper. "I like Dave. Way down deep inside, I'll admit to a little more than *like* at this point, but I won't do that to myself, not when I know better."

Mom patted the seat beside her. "Come sit." When Lisa complied, Mom put an arm around her shoulders and tucked her close. She didn't say anything for several seconds. When Lisa glanced up through her lashes, she could tell her mom was praying. She added her own silent request. *Jesus, I need your wisdom I asked Dave to give me a couple of days, but there's no way my answer can be anything but no...is there?*

"Sweetheart, your father was a very driven man. He accomplished so many great things for God, but he gave up a lot in the process. Things I didn't like, things he could never get back, and things that left a sour taste in your mouth. I'm not going to take up for him, I did enough of that while he was alive."

"Why did you put up with it? I mean you just always followed right behind him like you agreed with what he was doing."

Mom gave the question some thought before she answered. "Love, I guess, and in a lesser measure, security. What would it have benefited us if I had refused to go with him? He wouldn't have been a part of our lives at all then. At least this way, we got the left overs of his time."

"And that stunk."

"I won't disagree with you," Mom said. "But I'll share what I've learned. Some people are called to the ministry, and that's all they should do. They just aren't wired for anything else. That was your father. He loved us, but we were never his first love." She squeezed Lisa's shoulders. "But I met a lot of ministers in our travels and ninety-nine out of a hundred of them combined their ministry and their family seamlessly."

"But, what if—?"

"Hush now. What ifs don't get us much. There's only one question that needs an answer today."

Lisa pulled away from her mother and studied her expectantly.

"Do you like this young man?"

"More than I thought it was possible to like anyone after just four weeks." Lisa's response held no hesitation.

"Then let me give you some Scriptures to read. Proverbs 3:15-17. Solomon is encouraging his child to seek wisdom. Pay special attention to verse seventeen. I think you'll find part of your answer there."

Lisa glanced at her watch. *Time to get moving.* She stood. "Thanks Mom. I'm going to go look that up. I'll be ready to go in an hour or so." Once Lisa was in her own room, she pulled out her Bible and read the whole third chapter of Proverbs. Her mom was right. Verses fifteen through seventeen told her exactly what she should do. Calm settled over her as she read Solomon's words about seeking wisdom aloud.

"She is more precious than rubies: and all the things thou canst desire are not to be compared to her. Length of days is in her right hand: and in her left hand riches and honor. Her ways are ways of pleasantness, and all her paths are peace."

Lisa closed the Bible and her eyes. "Father, You know my heart. You know what I fear, but more than that, You know what I need even when I can't see it for myself. I'm asking You for wisdom to make a good choice...the right choice. I've been looking for my future, and maybe I've ignored what You've put in front of my face. I haven't asked You about Dave, because I eliminated him from the equation the moment he mentioned the ministry. It's just so scary to see the same things when I look back and when I look forward. I don't want to hurt either of us, but I do want your will. That pleasant and peaceful path that only wisdom can reveal to me." She kept her eyes closed for a few minutes, waiting for God to drop that more-precious-than-rubies nugget into her heart. When the answer came, it was no less than what she'd expected.

DAVE PAUSED on the threshold of his pastor's home office. Noah Tate hadn't noticed his arrival yet, and Dave took the few seconds to study the man and the room. At nearly eighty, the old man still carried himself straight as a stick. Age had left his round face a little heavy in the jowls and stolen most of the hair from his head, but the eyes behind the glasses were sharp, knowing, and compassionate. The room was nothing less than a library of theological reference books and notebooks filled with sermon notes spanning a fifty-five year old ministry. Even from the doorway, Dave could see colored notes sticking out from them like quills on a porcupine. There wasn't anyone in this world that Dave wanted to pattern his life after more than Noah Tate. He knocked on the door to gain the old man's attention.

"Oh, Dave. Come in, son, come in. Close the door if you would."

Dave did as the old pastor bid and took a seat in one of the comfortable, worn arm chairs that faced the desk.

Pastor Tate followed Dave's progress across the room with his eyes and, when the younger man sat, looked at him with an unreadable expression. His sigh was heavy as he took out a handkerchief, removed his glasses, and polished them under the desk light.

With the glasses removed, Dave could see a weariness in the man's gray eyes that hadn't been there a week ago. He guessed that was normal, given the circumstances. The building the storm had destroyed was only ten years old. Dave hadn't been here during that building program, but he'd heard the stories of how this man had worked day and night for months doing grunt work early and late to move the project along. He looked at the odd angle of the man's left wrist, which he'd been told had been caused by a fall from a ladder during that time. The sight straightened Dave in his seat. He made a promise to himself, then and there, to do whatever he could to lessen Noah Tate's burden as they rebuilt Abundant Life.

The old gentleman slipped his glasses back into place. "Terrible thing yesterday. I can only give God praise that the town had enough warning to take shelter. The property loss is great, but lives were spared, thank God." He tilted his head. "I heard you rode out the storm in a closet."

"Yes, sir. It's not an experience I'd like to relive, but God had his hand over us."

Noah Tate nodded. "I'm glad you're OK." He seemed to hesitate over his next words. "Dave, I want you to know what a pleasure it's been to work with you over the last year. Watching you grow in the Lord has reminded me of my own early days. Thank you for that."

Dave swallowed, appreciating the praise but afraid of where this conversation might be going. "Thank you, sir. You've taught me a lot."

"That's good to hear." He rose and paced back and forth behind his desk. "I didn't get much sleep last night. Too much in my head and my heart. Lots of soul searching and even some arguing with my Heavenly Father about what comes next. I'm not entirely happy with the answer, but I understand it." He stopped and faced Dave. "I'm retiring."

The floor fell out from under Dave with those words. "Sir?"

"I'm not as young as I used to be. Another building project of this size just isn't in me. I would have pressed forward anyway, but God is telling me to leave this in the hands of a younger man. The argument was ugly, but I've always prided myself in following the path God had laid out for me. I can't backtrack on that now. When Abundant Life's congregation meets in Harold Anderson's barn this morning, it'll be to receive my retirement. I've apprised the board of the situation. They'll be looking for us a place to meet while the building is rebuilt, and they will be lining up candidates to fill the pulpit."

Dave swallowed, speechless.

The older man sat and folded his hands on the desk. "Now the hard part."

Hard part? Dave leaned forward.

"As you know, your appointment to the position of youth pastor was totally at my discretion, maintained by a reasonable give and take of working together. You've never let me down. I want you to know how much I appreciate that. But as I retire, the position you fill must be opened to the discretion and needs of the new leadership. I know your ministry with us has just been part time—"

"It's been much more than that to me."

There were tears in the old man's eyes when he continued. "I know that, Dave. Just like I know that God has big things planned for you down the road. Once the congregation installs a new pastor, I'll make sure he gets a glowing recommendation of your faithfulness and abilities, but I can't begin to guess what direction the church and its new leadership might take."

Dave understood everything the old pastor said, even agreed with ninety-eight percent of it. Didn't matter. He'd still had his life yanked out from under him. Even if it had been done with love, it still hurt.

Behold, I will do a new thing.

The words settled into his spirit. He completed the verse in his head. *Now it shall spring forth, shall ye not know it? I will even make a way in the wilderness, and rivers in the desert.*

God had a plan. Yes, the decision of his mentor gave him a reason to grieve in the present, but God's promise gave him a reason to hope for the future. *Thank You, Father.*

He the shook the elderly pastor's hand, promised to help in whatever way he could to make the time of transition easier, and left the office. Dave sat in his truck and mulled the verse. The words were like a present he could hold but couldn't open until permission was given. And just like a little kid, he turned it over and over, shaking it in an effort to discern the contents by the sound of the rattle. *Just a hint?* He grinned when the truck remained quiet. God wrapped a sturdy gift.

The ringing of his phone startled him. He sent a glance upward when he saw Lisa's name on the screen. He held it while it rang a second time. He'd agreed not to push, and she'd promised to call him when she'd worked some things out. The phone rang a third time, and still he hesitated. *Father?*

Answer it.

Dave swiped the call open doing his best to ignore the way his hands shook. "Hello."

"Yes!"

His lips ticked up. "Yes, what?"

"You're going to make me say it, aren't you?"

"I think it's only fair."

"You're just mean, but all right." Lisa's deep breath was audible over the connection. "Mom and I talked. God and I talked. I owe you an apology for trying to make you pay for someone else's mistakes. If you still want to go out with me, if you still feel like exploring a future with me, then I want those things too."

He didn't know exactly what God had in mind with His promise of *new things*, but if this was the first hint, he couldn't wait to unwrap the rest of that package.

EPILOGUE

12 MONTHS later

LISA SISKO PLANTED her feet wide on the porch of Mrs. Craig's new house while she twisted to work out the kink in the small of her back. She breathed deep of the scents of new wood and fresh paint and offered a thumbs-up to heaven. *You did good work here, Father. Please help those who are still struggling. Please help Dave in this season of change.*

She added herself to that prayer. She'd been jumpy and preoccupied for a few weeks and had no idea what was causing it. Maybe her husband's restlessness over the prolonged dry spell in his ministry was finally getting to her.

The year since the tornado had demolished their hard work had been filled with hills and valleys. That day last April had brokered changes in so many lives, some good and some bad. But as the months ticked off the calendar, progress was being made in Yellow Veil and Harrison. New homes, new buildings, and new businesses. Yellow Veil was even getting its own Sonic. It was makeover of heavenly proportions...except for Abundant Life Church, and she didn't understand.

She'd held Dave's hand in a barn filled with hay and folding chairs while Pastor Tate delivered his *morning after* resignation. She'd watched as Abundant Life's building program stalled for lack of leadership, and the faithful continued to meet in a rented store-front. Human confusion threatened to turn into doubt when each Sunday the store front number shrank as members found the stability they needed in the churches of the surrounding towns. The outlook was bleak, but Lisa refused to believe that God was done with Dave and Abundant Life Church.

I wish Daddy were here.

Lisa smiled at the recurring thought. The man hadn't been perfect by any means, but this situation suited his talents perfectly. He could have salvaged what the storm had left behind. She whispered the verse she'd memorized in those first days of loss. Romans 8:28. "And we know that all things work together for good to them that love God, to them who are called according to his purpose."

"I've always loved that verse."

Lisa jumped and turned to find that Mrs. Craig had joined her on the porch.

"When I get weary, it reminds me of who's in control." Mrs. Craig took a seat in a brand-new rocker. "I can't tell you how good it feels to be back in my own home." She motioned to her chair's twin. "Sit and tell me how that young man of yours is doing. I haven't seen him in a couple of weeks."

Lisa obliged. "He wanted to be here today to help move your stuff in, but the insurance agency is a bee hive just now. He's putting in sixty hour weeks more often than not."

Mrs. Craig waved Lisa's apology away. "How are things across the river?"

"The town is flourishing. Abundant Life, not so much. I have to accept that God sees and understands more than I can. Things will work out in His timing, not mine...or Dave's."

"It's a shame that Noah Tate felt the need to retire. Even more of a shame that his retirement put an early end to Dave's appointment." She stretched out an age gnarled hand and squeezed Lisa's.

"You hold onto that verse you were quotin'. God has a place and a plan for each of us. A young couple like the two of you, willing to dig in and get your hands dirty wherever there's a need like you did out here last spring... God won't let that go to waste for long."

"I don't think so either. Dave's helping Jemma at Praise Tabernacle on Wednesday nights."

Mrs. Craig slapped her knees. "There you go. I'm sure that brings him some joy, but I'll be praying. I think God has something special in store for the two of you."

Lisa looked down at her lap and couldn't help the little smile that tugged at her lips. The last year had been a challenge. She and Dave had married six months ago, a simple ceremony in the Tates' living room with Jemma and Lisa's mom as witnesses. They'd been so busy with projects in the adjoining communities, they hadn't even taken time out for honeymoon yet. But if what she suspected turned out to be fact, they were going to need some direction in their lives sooner rather than later. She glanced up and found Mrs. Craig studying her with knowing eyes. "I don't doubt that in the least," Lisa whispered.

DAVE LOOKED at the time display in the bottom right corner of his computer. How could it possibly be six-fifteen? *Lisa will strangle me if I'm late for dinner one more night this week.* He sorted papers into three piles for attention tomorrow. He hated leaving the work undone, but he hated putting a frown on Lisa's face more. He moved his mouse over to the power icon, prepared to shut the computer down. The chime for an incoming message sounded before he could click the button.

He blew out a breath. It was probably the response he was waiting for on the Murdock claim. It could wait until tomorrow, but if the news was what he expected, taking the time to pass a blessing along to a patient and deserving couple would brighten his day as well as theirs.

Dave clicked on the message. He slumped back in the chair before he'd finished half of it and immediately straightened. This had nothing to do with the Murdock claim, but it was good news, it was great news...at least for him. He had no idea how Lisa would categorize it.

Yellow Veil was their home now. Her Mom lived just across the bridge. He had a steady job... Wouldn't asking her to consider a move put him in the same category as her father? He read the message a second time and felt something dormant stirring in his heart.

Father, if this is Your will, make a way.

Dave dashed off a quick response and printed out the message. He needed to talk with his wife, and he didn't need her irritated because he was late. The twenty-minute drive home seemed a lot shorter with so many questions and possibilities crowding Dave's mind, and under it all his prayer echoed. *Your will, Father, Your will,*

He lost his nightly race with Chester, let himself in the house, stooped to pat the purring Snowflake, and followed his nose to the kitchen just in time to see Lisa taking a meatloaf out of the oven. "That smells like heaven."

Lisa whirled, the pan clutched between two pot holders. "Oh, good grief!" Don't sneak up on me like that."

"Sorry, sweetheart, I wasn't sneaking, at least not intentionally."

Lisa sent him a narrow-eyed look that quickly turned into a smile. "Don't mind me, I've had a long day. We got Mrs. Craig all settled, had a nice visit on her porch. She's so happy to be back home..."

While Lisa babbled, Dave eyed the meatloaf and the foil-wrapped baked potatoes and the baked beans that already occupied the table next to homemade rolls and a salad. Curiosity peaked. All of his favorite dishes in one meal, and a wife that seemed as jumpy as a cat. He had something to share, it was pretty obvious that she did too.

He waited for her to put the hot pan on the table before pulling her into is arms. He kissed her hello, surprised when she responded with more emotion than the simple gesture normally received. Dave bundled her closer. "What's up, babe?

Lisa giggled and dodged out of his arms. "Nothing, silly. Like I said, just an interesting afternoon." She motioned for him to take a seat. "Did you have a good day?"

Dave studied her for a second before taking his seat. She wasn't upset nervous, so the car and the checkbook must be in good shape. But there was something on her mind. One thing his wife was not was shy. She'd work her way around to whatever it was in due time.

"It was just a day. More claims, more policies, more questions about delayed payments."

Lisa cut the meatloaf, lifted out a generous serving, and placed it on Dave's plate. He frowned at the slight tremor in her hands.

"I can't believe there are still people waiting for claims to be payed after a year. It's not like the company can dispute any of the storm damage." She held out a hand and waited.

"It's your turn," Dave reminded her.

"Oh, yeah." Lisa bowed her head. "Jesus, thank you for the meal You've provided. Thank You for watching over us every day. Thanks for...new challenges and blessings. Amen."

Dave shoved his plate to the side. "OK, I'm not eating a single bite until you tell me what is going on."

"Nothing, I..."

He crossed his arms and gave her his I'm-not-kidding look.

"OK," she huffed, but she looked more excited than annoyed. She scooted back from the table, opened a cabinet, and brought out two wrapped gifts. Dave frowned when she handed them to him.

"It's not my birthday, and our anniversary is six months away."

"Just open them." She tapped the larger of the two. "Start with this one."

Dave set the smaller gift on the table and ripped the paper off the flat rectangular box. He studied the contents, at a loss for words and meaning. "These are copies of my resume. I don't understand."

"You will when you open the second box."

He kept his gaze glued to hers as he reached for the remaining gift. The box was small, not much room for anything in there. When the box came open he looked at the blue-and-white plastic stick in confusion, frowned at Lisa, and looked back to the stick. "What...?" Reality almost knocked him out of his chair. "Ohhh..." He drew the word out on a long exhale before he looked back at his wife.

"A baby?"

She nodded. "Surprise."

Dave leapt from his seat, pulled Lisa to her feet, and crushed her to him. "Oh, wow. This is the best day of my life. When?"

"In about seven months. I made an appointment at the doctor for next week. They'll be able to give us a date."

Dave just nodded, unable to speak for the emotion that clogged his throat.

Lisa took a step away and tapped the first gift. "You're gonna need to get these in the mail, ASAP."

Dave studied her, his heart beating out of his chest. "Why?" The question carried more than just his hopes.

Lisa's eyes filled. "You're restless, I'm restless, and we're starting a family. You weren't called to sell insurance, and something tells me that our future isn't in Yellow Veil or Harrison. If God's trying to push us out of the nest, it's time to find out where He wants us."

"I think I might have a clue about that." Dave reached into his pocket and pulled out the folded printout from his computer. He handed it to Lisa and moved to re-read it over her shoulder, amazed at God's perfect timing.

Dear Mr. Sisko, We hope this note finds you in good health. You submitted your resume to us a couple of years ago, but at that time we felt God leading us in another direction. That situation has changed. We reached out to your former pastor, and he had nothing but great things to say about your dedication to service. Our current youth pastor is taking a new position in another state. We have a thriving youth program and were hoping that you might be inter-ested in visiting with us about the position. Please contact us at your earliest opportunity.

Lisa looked up, laughter dancing in her eyes. "This came today?"

"Yep."

She looked back down at the sheet of paper. "I was thinking earlier about makeovers." She laid a hand on her flat belly. "God made over my attitude, now He's making over our family and our future." She turned in Dave's arms and met his smile with one of her own. "Garfield, Oklahoma, huh?

He nodded. "Only if you want to give it a try as much as I do."

"I think it sounds like a wonderful place to raise a family."

DEAR READER

Thanks so much for choosing A MAKEOVER MADE IN HEAVEN. It's always a treat for me when God allows me to revisit the characters of Valley View. This one was especially fun since Dave and Lisa's story was my first attempt at a straight romance. If you enjoyed reading it as much as I enjoyed writing it, I'd love a review if you are so inclined.

While you wait for that next story to perk, I'd be honored if you'd check out some of my other stories. I've listed them for you on the next page. I write about ordinary women with extraordinary faith. You'll find plenty of romance, a dash of humor, more than a little friendship, and even a few tears as my characters meet real life head on and come out on top with God by their side.

Thanks again!

Sharon

NEVER MISS A NEW RELEASE. SIGN UP FOR MY NEWSLETTER AT SHARONSROCK.COM

ACKNOWLEDGMENTS

Father, thank You for one more idea, and the words to see it through to the end. I hope it turned out the way You wanted.

Lacy, You took the helm when my rudder was broken and steered me true until you were sure I could steer myself. (Deuteronomy 31:12)

Marian Merritt, Robin Patchen, Judy Devries, and Elizabeth Lopez: Thank you for taking my words and polishing them to a high shine. I couldn't...wouldn't want to make this journey without you!

CPSIA information can be obtained
at www.ICGtesting.com
Printed in the USA
BVHW031704020720
582866BV00001B/163

9 781723 449086